Six Seeds

Pantheon Reborn: Book 1

Tamara Natasha

Special Thanks

To my husband, Cory, and my shining moon, Jayde, who always support any creative pursuit I have. Thank you so much for believing in everything I do. The love you have for me inspires the drive to show that level of love in everything I do.

To my sister, Kyndra. To my Found Family and my Faire Family, of which there are many to name, who always cheer me on and inspire me with their own creativity.

Finally, to my kids: Owen, Lake, and Blade. You are all going to grow up to be amazing story tellers. I cannot wait to hear all the ones you have to tell.

Prologue

One would think the god of the dead would enjoy the darkness and chill that came with the domain of the Underworld. It was a misconception that Hades did not openly dismiss, although his attitude often showed he clearly wasn't enjoying himself. The god felt the place was dismal, depressing, and haunting.

There was little pleasure to be found in punishing the wicked. The ever increasing number of people being punished simply served to remind him of the world's growing wretchedness. A cruel reminder that some of the most monstrous beings were very human. All punishment did was embitter them and very rarely did any of them see the error of their ways. Such beings certainly were not going to be rewarded with peace.

Unlike those in Tartarus, the souls that were innocent and good were given peace in the Elysian Fields. It was a reprieve from pain. A reward for somehow managing to keep valor and hope in themselves even when temptations to do wrong were great. It was the least he could do after all when he knew some of the people there were hurt by those who were being punished for their crimes.

Hades was always busy with souls so he rarely left his realm. He made sure they were cared for or punished. However, there were moments he took advantage of leaving when his presence was called for. Short lived moments, but he was still a slave of duty. He took pride that he did his job properly at the very least, even though at times he envied the careless way his brother flounced about. All of the mess and chaos Zeus made reminded Hades as to why he seldom went about causing trouble. The temptation to traipse about with wanton abandon was still there. Perhaps trade with someone in a deal for them to take over his job and free him to do whatever he wished.

Except Hades knew all too well that a lesser person would probably disrupt everything. The afterlife was just as precarious as life itself. Souls had rest, punishment, or in some rare occasions were given a chance to live again through reincarnation. To entrust anyone else to such a job was unthinkable. Even if he growled and grumped about and made it near impossible for the dead to come back to life.

Hades did soon discover his world did not always have to be so dark. A woman he swept away had become his light and warmth. What had begun as a moment of selfishness to no longer wake in a bed with no one beside him had turned into discovering his heart still raced. That cold organ in his chest felt as though it had caught on fire as he got to know the woman named Kore. She had refused to eat or drink anything of his realm in fear of being trapped there forever. The god could not bring himself to blame her even a little.

While he desperately had not wanted to be left alone again, he left the choice up to her. If she at least stayed for a little while and allowed him to properly learn a little of her, he could survive whatever choice she made. In his world, there was rarely ever a chance to be able to meet someone as lively as she was. In his world, he also knew what it meant to be caged. He certainly would not allow for her to be trapped against her will. Soon enough it seemed that her time with him came to a swift end when her mother arrived to take her back.

There had been a small hope returned to him when he discovered that Kore had chosen to eat of the food in his realm. Hope and shock and filled him as he realized pomegranate seeds that were left upon her tongue that counted to six seeds. Her mother, Demeter, was furious and threatened an eternal barren winter upon the world if she did not get her daughter back. Through Zeus, a painful compromise was made, for six months of the year he could have his beloved Kore at his side. The world would be harsh and cold because of it, and for six months of the year she would be gone from his sight and his world would be without light.

For his beloved Kore, he would give her whatever she wished. Her name became Persephone, and he could see how she adored the word upon his lips when he greeted her when she came home to him. She became his Queen, his lover, and light. Someone worth the wait. Yet as the world changed, those months always felt as though they dragged on. He felt restless more and more with every year that passed that they had to say goodbye to each other when they did not want to. The six months were all too short.

Hades wished to find a way for her to be free to choose to stay or go whenever she pleased. He wanted to be able to come and go from this realm as he wished too. Determination filled him at the very idea of freedom. There was no doubt he could devise a plan, but the question was if he would be the cost of such freedom.

1

"Doctor Melanthios, Officer Bowet is here. She found an abandoned litter of puppies and an injured feral cat." The voice was cool and deliberate through the intercom of the phone. It sounded loud in the small office located in an enclosed patio that overlooked a large garden that had a chain-link fence. The garden itself was the dog-run that was currently being showered in the golden sunlight that filtered through creamy sheer curtains. The room glowed with a peaceful warmth that seemed at home with the sounds of dogs barking and cats meowing and the clicking of the keyboard.

The doctor looked up from his notes he was transcribing to study the intercom. One hand moved to adjust the rimless glasses as he flipped through his schedule. An absent biting of his bottom lip while he thrummed his fingers against the desk. He finally pressed the button on his phone and spoke to it.

"Please have them sent to the examination room, Mr. Charoni . I will be there momentarily. Ask if Miss Dawzey will take a slightly later appointment for Franklin. If not, I will do my best to see to her and our newcomers."

"Of course, Doctor Melanthios." The click of the humming intercom being turned off made the room go quiet and the man stood and stretched. He smoothed out his dress shirt and folded his glasses and set them aside before picking up the small badge from his desk and clipping it onto his collar. On it was a small picture that he thought looked terrible. It made tanned skin look grey and his long black hair look like a shadowy ink blot. The light even glared off his glasses that he had forgotten to take off. It made him look like some sort of alien. By now, it was something he just accepted. It wasn't what was important anyway.

Tahvo Melanthios made his way from the door of his office and down the hall to a small prep room where he pulled on his white lab coat and washed his hands all the way up to his elbows thoroughly. A check to make sure his implements were sealed as they ought to be and he did a quick check of the room before entering an adjoining room where his assistant performed an initial check of vitals of a lethargic feline. Meanwhile the Animal Control officer was assisting with the puppies, making sure they were settled and fed.

The one looking over the cat was James Cheroni, the same man who had given voice over the intercom. His skin was a dark ashen brown and hair was in cornrows tight against his head. He wore a white coat with blue scrubs and a nametag with a photo of questionable quality on it as well.

He had a willowy build that made him sometimes seem as though he would vanish if you looked away.

The officer in the room was a woman with light brown skin and dark burgundy hair pulled back in a bun. Her uniform was a drab olive green shirt and khaki slacks. She was built wide and tall, someone who could handle any sized animal with ease. There was a certain elegance about Officer Bowet that commanded authority and respect.

"What nightmares have you pulled these guys from?" Tahvo asked as he looked over the dirty calico sedated on the towel covering the metal table. He pulled on gloves and started to look it over. He could see the teeth marks on the body. Frankly, she was lucky to be alive. Aside at first glance of flesh wounds what seemed like a few damaged ribs, the cat just seemed mostly hurt and starving.

"Nightmare." Bowet corrected him, "Locals said a car hit the mother a while ago. I am guessing the cat was nursing them for a while until a coyote tried to get at them. She saved these little guys. I have the coyote in the back of my vehicle while he naps. She gave him a hell of a time. If you have it handled here, I am going to make sure he gets properly relocated."

"Of course. Thank you, Cecilia." Tahvo went back to look over the cat. Frowning as he looked her over. Poor thing looked worse for wear, but the little feline had a hell of a fighting spirit.

"James, could you please clean up our brave friend? I would like to make sure she doesn't get any infections before we do anything else."

There was a silent nod from the other male who carefully picked up the cat with a practiced care. Meanwhile the puppies were inspected and checked over. Three small pups who badly needed a bath as much as the cat did. Very new to the world and he was certain they were a mixed breed. Tahvo carefully went through the effort to clean each one and give a second look over them. Each one got their first vaccines and were even fed and coddled until they fell into a content slumber.

He carefully moved them into a small quiet kennel with a padded pet bed with a baby monitor left on so he could hear them if they needed to be fed again shortly. Soon after that he checked over the little hero when James brought her in.

"I think you are going to need some rest little Callie." Tahvo said softly as he tucked her into a kennel right beside the pups after doing all he could to ensure her health and comfort for the time being. Taking time to ensure their comfort, he washed up and moved onto the next examination room to a small dog named Franklin and his human, Miss Dawzey.

The woman was a short one who cuddled the small trembling dog against her chest as she waited. The aging dog was a pleasure to always check on. Doctor Melanthios smiled lightly at them both as he held his hands out for the small dog. He remembered the first time he met the woman. She had been petrified of the tall looming male with the resonating voice. Yet she discovered that he truly was not as scary as he appeared. At least not to her. The dog liked him and the appointment had gone smoothly.

Now the woman handed over her little dog with ease and the vaccinations and check up went well. The older dog was starting to show signs of age on the russet muzzle. Slightly sunken eyes and little dashes of white fur. A small treat for Franklin who gobbled it up. Tahvo smiled to the woman.

"Everything looks just fine with Franklin, Miss Dawzey. Thank you for waiting patiently." He said.

"Oh, no problem. I know you are awfully busy here. With me moving soon, I wanted to get one last check up with you before we go. Did you have any recommendations for good vets in Arlington?" She pet her small dog as she moved him into the small purse like dog carrier that had a plush little pillow inside of it.

"I know several in fact. I can make sure Mr. Cheroni gives a list to you on your way out."

"Thank you, Doctor Melanthios. We appreciate it very much. I am sorry I cannot bring anymore plants to the Elysian Fields clinic. I do know a very good place though that is just a few blocks from here. It is a beautiful shop."

She started to dig around in her wallet and picked through receipts and business cards until she found what she wanted. Blue eyes lit up and she held out the card to him, "There we are. Seraphic Plant Nursery. It is new"

He took the card and looked it over. It wasn't too far away from the clinic. It was certainly worth a shot. Tahvo thanked her and held the door for her as she left before checking on the new puppies and Callie. It looked like it was time to eat. Most of the day was spent in that manner, nursing puppies, helping the cat, and taking appointments. It was after the last appointment that Tahvo gave another bit of food for the puppies before calling James over the intercom.

"James, could you please remain to observe our new guests before you leave for the night? I am going to take Spot out for his evening walk."

"Yes, Doctor Melanthios." He answered. Deliberate and clear again to ensure there would be no way one could misunderstand him over the intercom. He was certain James would be understood in a rioting storm. Tahvo waited until James slipped in and claimed one of the comfortable chairs in the room. A laptop was with him for paperwork. Tavho gave a soft sound of thanks before he stepped out to hang up his lab coat and went down the hall to his office.

The man stepped out through the glass doors to the deck that made a wide walkway. Along the outside of the fence that protected the run in the spots the clinic didn't frame it. Only his office and the door that led to the dog kennels opened into it. He walked along the deck path, one could see a much larger area with several fenced off areas and stables. For those, he had hired help to help upkeep them after he checked on all of the large animals. He sadly could not be everywhere at once.

A little further and he stepped off onto a cobblestone path leading up to a large two story home. Much like the rest of the land, it had trees and plant life surrounding it. Everything felt alive and welcoming. It was certainly something he preferred. He stepped through his front door to be greeted by the scuffling of feet. He may have lived alone, but there was a reason his house was so large.

The first one to greet him was a massive black great dane whose shoulder was at Tahvo's hips as the dog rammed said shoulder into him in greeting and circled around him in excitement. He knew exactly what time it was after all. Tahvo laughed softly and pet the dog. Fingers working into the short fur behind the ears while that tail whipped through the air.

"Who is a good Spot?" He asked cheerfully as he knelt down and ruffled the furry scruff around his shoulders Spot licked his face, "Yes, that would be you. We are going to go for a walk and get some things for some new friends. We have a brave cat and some puppies."

In his house the patients that needed far more intensive care for feedings tended to stay in his house for a bit. Made it easier for night feedings, administering medicine, and changing bandages. He took great care in making sure any animal that came into his clinic was made comfortable.

Spot wagged his tail harder as soon as he heard the word friends. Another giant lick over Tahvo's face again before bolting off to go and grab his leash off the little blunt hook that was set low. The dog trotted back over expectantly with the bright blue and reflective silver leash. Sitting down, he let his human take the leash and clip the end onto metal ring on his collar. As soon as his human stood up, the hound did too and trotted just a step behind so that his owner could lead him out the front door and down to the brick-paved driveway that winded down to the street the clinic was on. He loved the way his trimmed claws clicked on the driveway.

The sun painted the sky brilliant pastels of oranges to blues and greens as it set. Tahvo scrolled through his phone to put on music and tucked it into his pocket as he hooked his headphone over one ear. Leaving the other open to hear his surroundings. It was a quiet and peaceful evening. Very little made him feel more content after a busy day of successfully helping animals than a walk with his dog outside in the quiet outskirts of the small town of Pius.

It was getting to the end of summer and he could tell with the slight tinges of yellow on the greens of some plants and the cool air that snaked through the soft breeze. The soft scratch of claws of Spot's claws on the sidewalk was a comfort as he made the long walk with his dog. His larger than normal Great Dane had once been the runt of his litter. A tiny black spot within a bunch of spotted puppies. Needless to say, he helped the pup thrive and fell in love with his companion and discovered the dog sprouted from all of that attentive care.

It was dogs like him that made Tahvo work hard to ensure others could thrive and grow. To hopefully find homes with people who could care just as much. If nothing else, they generally found a home with him and the clinic. Not that he particularly minded. It certainly kept him from being lonely. He paused as he saw the sign for the plant nursery and studied the flowers currently climbing along its walls like a living frame. Ah, so this was where it was. He absently pet his dog as he studied the sign and then looked up the short stepping stone path to catch sight of someone knelt down by the flower bed nestled at the front of the shop. Its picture windows were decorated with swirling paint depicting vines and flowers framing name of the shop. The other large window had a sign hanging on it offering discounts for landscaping for their opening week.

The woman working there had vibrant green and blue hair that was sticking out through the hole in her baseball cap and along the brim. That brilliant hair stood out even more against the brown overalls. He found himself trying to just get a better look at her before he felt a jerk of the leash and Spot dragged him towards the woman who was digging a hole in the ground to transfer a plant from a pot.

"Ack! Spot, no! Heel!" Tahvo called loudly as he had to keep from being toppled forward, "Cerberus! I said stop!" He watched the dog skid to a stop and wag his tail at the woman looking at him. Suddenly he felt like the air went out of his lungs as he saw the most intense pair of light brown eyes that nearly looked gold in the sunlight. Laughter filled them as he watched her remove her gloves and hold her hand out to the dog so that he could sniff her hand.

"You know, most people ask the owner if they can try to put their hand to the dog. He could be the kind to bite." Tahvo found himself speaking in a terse tone without thinking. Did he really mind? Not really, but it did not change that he said it. He then cringed as the woman drew her hand back and her face screwed up,

"Not that Spot will bite you. He is actually quite pleasant." He amended quickly. Wow, he was so much better with animals than people.

She still hesitated until the dog stepped forward that last foot between them and he licked her face. That made her giggle and Tahvo felt like his heart crawled up into his throat at the sound. When she finally laid her eyes on him, he shifted under the scrutiny. When her bright eyes met his, he went so very still. He felt like one wrong move would end... something. Not that he entirely was sure what he was suddenly panicking over, but the woman studying him with an unreadable expression was daunting.

Breathe. He could do it. Truly. Finally, he cleared his throat and squat down so that he could be on eye level with her and to pet his all too pleased dog, "My name is Tahvo. This is Spot. Or Cerberus when he is in trouble." He suddenly gave all too much focus to the black fur as she gave a blessed giggle to his words. The sound made his head buzz with distant whispers and it scattered coherent thought.

"My name is Lyric. Happy to meet you. I am glad Spot is so sweet. I bet he thought I was playing in the dirt and wanted to join me." She mused as she scratched under Spot's chin. Those light browns went to study Tahvo as he tried very hard not to look at her. Was he shy or was he one of those people who just seemed better at speaking to animals than people?

"I like his name when he is in trouble though. I think it is very fitting for him." Lyric found that she really liked the warmth of the golds streaking through the vivid green eyes of this Tahvo character. The cool tanned skin and black hair just seemed to make them ever brighter as she could see just how much he loved the silly dog he stared at so hard. The hound seemed like an anchor as though the man would worry he would just fall away.

Lyric. When she said her name, he could tell it simply fit. Her voice was almost sing-song with its soothing notes. He truly had no idea how she sent him into such an awkward silence. Usually he had no problem talking to someone in at least a professional manner. Formalities seemed too... cold with her kneeling there with melting his dog with thorough attention. This really should not have been ter-ribly difficult.

Finally he worked up the nerve to look at her and realized that she was studying him again with that thoughtful scruti-ny. He swore if she kept that up, that he would be con-vinced that she would see right through him. Something needed to be said before she was able to do so.

"I think your name is very fitting for you." He managed and then felt his cheeks go hot as she stared him for that blurted thought. He put his face in his hand as she started to giggle. It was almost enough to cause him to wilt. His pride certainly was as he tried to figure out a way to salvage this. Possibly. A groan escaped as he mentally kicked himself.

Lyric looked at the man sympathetically and finally stifled her giggles to lean forward and kiss the dog on his muzzle, "Well, Spot, I think your human is very sweet. You better take good care of him. If you are a good boy and wait right there, I will finish planting this chrysanthemum and then get you a treat." A look towards the hiding male, "That is, of course, it is okay with you, Tahvo."

In an effort not to say anything else horrifically embarrass-ing, Tahvo nodded a little and just found himself sinking fingers into the scruff while she dug a little deeper into the soil. A soft hum coming from the bright-haired woman as she worked. He watched as she tucked the plant into the ground and pushed the dirt in around the knot of dirt and roots. A gentle pat and a little water before she stood up and brushed herself off. It was a futile action, given her hands and face were covered in nearly as many smudges of dirt that disguised some of the scattering freckles over her cheeks.

He really did want to stand when she did, but he found his legs refused to work. A stare as she patted Spot before slipping into the front door and vanishing into the shop. While she was gone, he looked down at the shameless dog that just gave him a doggy grin with his tongue hanging out of his mouth. Whip like tail wagged and thumped the ground with near impatience.

"What in the world possessed you to bolt, boy?" Tahvo murmured. His hands absently smoothing the fur. It helped him not feel the crushing weight of feeling awkward. He almost felt like he could stand up again right until Lyric returned with a potted plant and a large treat that looked to be homemade. He knew the plant immediately; rosemary. A plant that was safe for dogs in particular.

"Here you go. This will help him stay nice and healthy and a treat just for the very good boy." She held the treat out for Spot to sniff until he delicately took it from her hand and then chomped it. Head ducking down as the pieces fell and he busied himself eating. She then held the plant out to Tahvo, "This is for you. I know some dogs like to chew on plants. I figured this would be a good one for him. As a thank you for letting me pet your adorable dog."

For him? Really? Tahvo stared at her before he willed himself to speak. He finally pushed himself to his feet and realized he was a head taller than her, "Ah, you don't have to. I would be more than happy to pay for it. I actually was coming to see what you had here. I have a litter of puppies and a cat that I was looking into getting some things for."

A thoughtful sound as Lyric studied him at the semi-refusal and then smiled brightly as she pulled something out of her pocket and held it out to him, "I thought you would say something like that. So, instead of my original plan of asking you out to dinner, would you be horribly embarrassed if I asked to come over to your place tomorrow night? I could bring some things for them too." She beamed brightly. No hesitation from the woman as she continued to hold out the fold of paper to him.

Tahvo had to process all of those words as he very slowly took the paper first and he opened it and blinked at the messy handwriting that had her name and phone number. Did he just get asked out for a date? It wasn't his first date by far, simply that he rarely had any interest beyond a few people that had been a night out for pleasure's sake. How many years had it been?

"Ah, yes, let me... ah... I don't have a pen." He frowned and then dug into his back pocket for his wallet and pulled out a card and held it out to her, "The large house behind the clinic is mine. Just follow the stone driveway beside the clinic and keep going past the fencing until you get to the house."

Scanning the words over the card, Lyric smiled brighter and nodded cheerfully, "Of course, Doctor. I will be there tomorrow. I am betting about Seven or Eight is good, yes?" When he nodded she folded her hands behind her back and stepped back after handing him the plant and knelt down to pet Spot, "I wish I had a dog like you. I bet all the digging would let me plant all sorts of things."

Spot woofed and licked her hand and rammed his shoulder into her lovingly before rounding about his human's legs and then trotting a bit down the path away expectantly. It was time to walk more! He watched his human as he hurriedly tucked the paper into his pocket and held the yummy plant in his other arm. Another woof as he paused and wagged his tail. His human seemed stuck there. Maybe he needed a good tug... or was he just thinking again?

"I might have a dog you will like. I run the shelter as well, and they do need a good home." Tahvo offered softly. Seeming unsure about leaving. Why did the idea of stepping away from the woman he just met suddenly make him feel dread? "I will see you tomorrow night then. Until then... it has been a pleasure meeting you, Miss Helios." He dipped his head politely and forced himself to take that first step away from her.

Every step hurt a little less and made it easier to breath in one way and difficult in an entirely different way. Tomorrow he had a date. A date with an all too charming and colorful woman. A glance back was stolen as he saw she was cleaning up her tools. A small smile finally started to tug on the corners of his lips as he walked with Spot back to his house. While he was nervous that he would make an utter fool of himself, he also was rather excited for this date.

He just prayed to whatever powers out there that it went well. Tahvo wasn't sure if he would survive embarrassing himself further than he already had. He caught Lyric glancing over her shoulder towards him right as his shoe caught the raised corner of sidewalk and he stumbled. The breeze was cruel and carried her attempts of stifled giggles to his ears as his face burned.

How in the world was he going to survive tomorrow night?

2

He had a date. *A date*! Tahvo stared at the clock in his kitchen as he stirred the noodles one last time. Soon Lyric would be coming over for dinner. One that he had managed to agree to. There had been such a haze in his mind as he worked the entire day since they agreed yesterday. Everyone was cared for to his best ability, but there were moments of pause he thought back to that brilliant blue and green hair and those bright near-golden eyes. The sound of her laughter was almost like a haunting dream.

Never was there ever a word for what he felt the moment his eyes had met hers. It was like he was suddenly handed an all too fragile piece of glass and just one wrong step would mean he would drop it and watch it shatter before him. Needless to say, he was panicking inside while moving about the kitchen. Checking over the sauce also on the stove and then checking the oven. Everything was timed as close together as possible. A way to keep busy and drown out the panic with tasks.

A deep breath as he went out to the dining room where he had a small round table that he had cleared his paperwork off of. A rich red table cloth spread over the table and a small centerpiece of an intricate flowering lantern with a flickering candle in it. He fussed with the utensils again and the glasses on the table before he heard a knock and nearly swept a glass off the table.

He wasn't jumpy at all. Nope. Spot trailed him all through the house, head canted whenever he saw his master jump and twitch at any sudden sounds. The doorbell rang next and he ran ahead to the door, barking in excitement as Tahvo came up behind him. Through the large etched window in the front door he could see the figure of the woman waiting for him. Although it did very little to prepare Tahvo for the way his heart stopped when he opened the door.

That green and blue hair was much more easily seen now with a zigzag part on her head bisecting the two colors and giving an interesting effect as she had it parted enough to the side for green pieces to fall into the blue. The curly hair fell to her hips. It was set off with the sheer brown blouse she wore over a black tank top and a pair of black loose swaying pants that hid all but the toes of brown boots. Without the overalls, he could see the sturdy build that he could admire. However, his focus were her eyes.

Stunned wasn't even the word for how he felt in that moment. Especially when she stood like a living piece of art in the doorway. Tahvo didn't want to simply admire her though. If he wanted that, he didn't need to have her over for dinner. He wanted to actually speak to her more than a few fumbled lines. Hopefully he could survive the night without fail. She deserved some decent conversation from him.

"Hello, Ms. Helios." A greeting after what he felt like was an eternity staring at her. Gods, she had to have thought he was an idiot. The date did not even begin yet. A move to slightly bow his head and offer his hand out to her, "I hope it had not been too hard to find my home."

There was a light of amusement in her eyes as she shifted the bag she had into her other hand and let him press his lips against her knuckles. A shot of warmth went up her arm. Lyric couldn't help but grin at him, "Lyric, please. Or else I will be calling you Doctor Melanthios all night and that just seems far too clinical."

That made his face go warm again as he stared at her for another moment, "I apologize. I am far more used to using a more professional form of address Miss He- ah, Lyric." He let her hand fall from his as he stepped back and watched Spot snuffle at her bag. Lyric held the bag up high and pet the pup before stepping into the foyer and holding the bag out to him.

"I brought you something for the puppies and the cat. Oh, and something for Spot." Lyric said. She watched him hesitate before finally accepting it. He took absolute care not to accidentally brush his fingers against her own. He was so very careful and exact in all of his actions. She noticed when he did something unintentional, he suddenly got so very flustered. Which was kind of cute when his green eyes lit up. Today, he wore a forest green shirt that seemed to just accent those eyes and a pair of light-colored slacks.

"Thank you. I am going to check on dinner, it should almost be done." He carefully cradled the bag and stood awkwardly. Should he lead her by hand? Offer an arm? What was the etiquette for a first date in your own home? Should they have done this in public? Actually, come to think of it he really would have rather they were far away from the public eye. If he made a fool of himself, then at least it would be in front of only one person and not an entire group of people.

After internal debate he finally started walking towards the living room, motioning for her to sit on the couch. Though he paused and looked a little apprehensive when he looked at it before finally speaking again, "I apologize for the dog hair. I don't like to keep Spot from laying on the sofa. That one is his favorite. So is the chair... and all of the furniture." He looked around the room. Everything was lightly coated with little black hairs on the dark grey and white plush furniture. One of the pillows had obviously seen better days as it was chewed on and stitched and patched up so much that it was hard to tell what the original color of it had been.

Lyric was about to say something to assure him it was really alright before the stove beeped loudly and she watched his alarmed eyes as the good doctor rushed out of the room. Leaving her alone with the cheerful dog that she swore was really a small horse. The woman smiled softly as she carefully went to pet Spot. He wagged his tail at her and then ran a tight circle around her legs before leaping onto his favorite sofa and sprawled his body over the entire length of it. Staring at her with intense eyes as he watched her. Lyric swore he was simply inviting her to look around the room.

After a long moment Lyric looked around the room and studied the walls. They were vibrant teal, allowing the greys and whites stand out against the cool color. The curtains were sheer and the blinds were rolled up high to allow sunlight into the room. The one wall was covered in shelves with a large collection of movies. Most of them disc format, but she spotted a few video tapes on the top shelf. Probably old favorites. The television was large and she could scarcely tell what remote she should use if she even did want to turn it on. It was a universal remote that she was entirely unfamiliar with.

She then moved to the wall full of pictures. A smile pulled on her features at the framed doctorate with a news clipping put in front of it. A far younger man standing in front of the clinic when it was new. The pride and hope in his features make her heart flutter. The photos surrounding it were all different animals. Ones she guessed that he must have saved. She found Spot. Given the date on the clipping, she realized that any photo on the walls in the living room were animals he helped. Some of them looked like photos he had with owners he found for them.

That smile grew when she heard music coming from another room. At first it was a loud and raucous music that she heavily suspected was some sort of heavy metal. A silence and then something punk. Then something in an unfamiliar language that almost covered his muttered curses. Then something romantic but... it was almost corny. Lyric couldn't help feed that curiosity when she went to find the source as she saw Tahvo trying to poke at his phone while it was connected to a set of speakers. Expression severe as he concentrated and fumbled trying to find the right kind of music. More mumbled curses as he tried to get technology to cooperate with him.

"I sometimes like jazz if that helps. Although, I do have a soft spot for rock and punk music depending on the mood." Lyric said. She watched him startle and he suddenly was juggling his phone in the air as he fought to keep gravity from taking it to the floor. Luckily, Tahvo won the challenge against gravity and the phone was safe from blunt force trauma for the time being,

"I am sorry." She offered, her words heavy with sincerity. He must have been incredibly on edge. Maybe he didn't interact with people outside of work often. Unless perhaps she was imposing. Had she misread him yesterday?

"Ah, it is alright. I was simply startled." He stammered and just set his phone down after a moment of hesitation. He was careful with his movements as went to the table and drew out a chair for her, "Dinner is ready. I just need to bring it out. Do you have any preferences in drinks? Wine, water, or tea?"

Please like one of those three, Tahvo thought to himself. Though he supposed he had juice in the fridge. He thought he did at least. He should have gone shopping the night before... or that morning.

"Tea would be wonderful, thank you Tahvo."

Lyric sat down and helped him push in her chair. He seemed to hesitate after, uncertain, before vanishing into the kitchen. She looked over the table and smoothed her fingers over the red tablecloth. Watching how the candle cast soft shadows from the cut metal on the lantern as it danced and flickered. With the sun setting, it was soon one of the main forms of light in the room aside from the dimmed lights that gave a cozy feel to the small dining table.

A look around and she realized the space that would have normally been used for a large table and perhaps a china cabinet instead had a corner desk with overhead shelves. A computer that was turned off and a printer and more little tables with all sorts of stacked paperwork and books. A lot of them, from what she could see, were about anatomy for various animals and others had diseases. He must have taken great care to research everything over and over for every animal he cared for. She was shaken from her thoughts as his phone went off with a piercing beep and she turned her head abruptly to the phone still connected to the speakers. With it amplified it was very loud and Spot started to bark from the other room.

There was a shattering sound and a curse in the kitchen that caused Lyric to start standing. That was until he rushed out. Two plates of food in his hands. He carefully set hers down in front of her and then set the other down at the other setting. His expression was dazed like he wasn't entirely seeing her there as he rushed over to the phone and turned off the alarm. A scowl tugged on his face as he pulled the phone off the cord and stuffed it into his pocket.

"I'm sorry, I need to... I need to go feed the puppies. And change." A dismal look down at his pants at the splash up from the feet up as he rubbed his neck. "Ah... you should eat before it gets cold. I'm sorry." His tone became clipped and he couldn't bring himself to look up at her as he briskly left the room and went up the stairs.

Lyric stared after him with wide eyes and finally blinked as she felt stunned and unsure. A look at the food and she picked at one of the noodles and ate it. Rotini noodles with chicken and a bacon alfredo sauce drizzled over it that she swore was made from scratch. He had to have worked so hard to make all of that. Quietly, she stood up and walked to the kitchen to see the mess made of what she figured must have been a glass pitcher filled with ice and tea and a few lemons spilled across the floor. Determined to help somehow, she went on a search for a dust pan and a mop.

Upstairs, Tahvo hadn't bothered to change yet as his first priority had been to make the formula for the pups as he settled down in front of them to carefully hold each one and feed them from a tiny bottle. Animals were so much easier to navigate. They had such very basic demands and for the most part if you filled those, they would be content with you. People were so much harder to deal with. He closed his eyes as he heard the soft padding of paws and felt the full lean of the black dog against his shoulder. The dog licked his cheek once before sprawling to curl around his back and study the puppies with a quiet interest.

"I've already made a fool of myself, Cerberus." Tahvo's voice quiet as he fed the puppy. The proper name for his hound was only ever used when he was upset. Fingers stroked against the top of the puppy's head as he did so. It wasn't like he was trying to be so jumpy. He never had this problem at work. Everyone always complimented him on how calm and in control he appeared to be. Some days he prided himself on that. He had no problems asking James for assistance or the rare passing chatter with Officer Bowet. Hell, perhaps he just fooled himself into thinking he could be a functioning human being. James Cheroni always made phone calls for him at work, a delegated task that he had thought nothing of until now.

He had always figured he would simply live out life alone with animals. It seemed a lot easier that way. Safer. Being around people... having to coexist with them beyond the safe barriers of work and the walls of his house? Terrifying.

Perhaps he would go downstairs and see that Lyric grew bored of waiting for him. He never thought he would care about how someone thought of him beyond a professional standpoint. Most people he shunted to the back of his mind. Except her, she was glaringly present in his mind as though he ought to make sure he would never forget her.

Now, he cared. Maybe it was just another thing on the list of things wrong with him. After all, he had just met her. There was no reason he should have been so worried about the opinion of a near stranger. Such thoughts ran through his head while Tahvo stared off into space as he carefully tucked the puppy beside the cat that demanded to sleep with the puppies. Very carefully he pulled another one out and proceeded to feed it as well. He could feel the soft nuzzle of Spot against his leg, reminding him that at least the dog's opinion of him would never change.

So focused on the puppy and his thoughts, he didn't hear as Lyric had finally found him in the room he was using to help care for the pups. It was a small bedroom that had a baby gate he left open. A soft pet bed and a bowl and fountain of water that was for the cat. It was a quiet and comfortable room for little baby animals. He couldn't see her as she studied him and carefully moved to sit down beside him. It wasn't until her leg touched his that he froze stiff. He didn't jump this time, as he didn't want to hurt the infant in his hands.

"Would you like any help, Doctor Melanthios?" Lyric's tone was careful and calm. The use of that name had their eyes meeting. Confusion clear in his expression and patience in her own.

She hadn't left? Honestly, he didn't understand it.

Tahvo frowned for a long moment before finally speaking, "I…" A look at the puppy in his hands and he carefully handed it over to her, "Yes. Please, Miss Helios. THEY will let you know when it is done eating." He carefully picked up the last one and the last little bottle he had for it. There was a hesitation before looking at her hands cradling the puppy before he realized there were bandages all over her fingers. Splotches of red on the woven bandages.

"Miss Helios, your hands–" Panic crept into his words.

"I couldn't find the dust pan, so I tried to pick up as much glass and ice as I could. It is hard to tell the difference sometimes." Lyric said quickly. A sheepish smile was paired with her admission and she wiggled her fingers a bit, "You might need to buy more paper towels too. I couldn't find a mop either. Or the rest of the paper towels. But it is all clean now… I think. I wouldn't let Spot walk down there just yet."

He gaped at before words escape in a strangled voice, "Miss Helios, I have a central vac system that also can clean wet messes." She could have kept from hurting herself. Why did she even go and clean it? He hadn't wanted to leave the mess, but the puppies had taken precedence in his mind. Now she was hurt by his negligence.

Now that... that had gotten Lyric's face to suddenly turn a bright red as she realized she had gone through a lot more trouble than required. If she had maybe asked first...

"Ah well, now I just feel incredibly silly. Well, at least Spot isn't going to accidentally get glass in his paws, right? I think I found every bit of it with my hands. Though I guess we should do another wipe down of the floor to be sure, huh?"

"I... I suppose .... Thank you, Miss Helios." The way her cheeks near glowed in embarrassment... it made those eyes glitter and shine, "You blush very prettily, Miss Helios." Tahvo found himself blurting without thinking again. As soon as the words left his lips he wanted to apologize.

Though suddenly he was silenced by a hand on his cheek. The warm calloused fingers cupping his face. Tahvo froze as Lyric gently moved to place the puppy she had finished feeding onto the bed before she shifted to move both of her hands to scoop up his well-fed pup so that they were all together. His cheek suddenly felt too cool without her hand there. That touch chased away the panic much like Spot did.

"Doctor Melanthios. Would it be so terribly... wrong for me to want to kiss you?" Lyric finally asked. She was studying the snuggling puppies and petting the purring feline when she voiced her thought.

"You wish to kiss me?" Did he slip on ice and hit his head? Was he suffering from a concussion? When she nodded, he noted that those cheeks lessened a little in their warmth, "Why?"

Well, now that was the five hundred dollar question. Lyric considered him for a long moment before speaking up, "Honestly? I think you are very attractive. You are also going through a lot of effort for just dinner with me and I've done nothing but giggle at you. I thought it was just nerves but... I feel like I have been mocking your struggle." Even if she didn't know what it was, "I don't want to romanticize something that could be painted as charming when you probably feel like anything but that. Even so, I find your care for detail touching. I just... want you to know that your efforts are appreciated."

Tahvo did not know what to say. Except he carefully curled his fingers under her chin, "I suffer from severe anxiety. Most days I can cope with medication. It allows me to function at work but... I have not been on a date in *many* years. Making dinner for someone else even more uncertain." He waited for her expression to turn dismayed. Instead it seemed to relax with understanding.

"Well, then please let me know what ways I can make it easier for you, Doctor Melanthios. I don't want to make you suffer through undue hardship because of me. A date should be fun, not stressful." Her voice soft as she looked up into those eyes that seemed to almost beg for understanding. They also showed a wish for him to be able to function without feeling so worried about every minute detail. "I came here to learn more about you, so if everything isn't absolutely perfect, that is alright. At least I get to enjoy it with you."

Such an astonishing woman that was sitting there beside him. Letting him hold her chin up with his hand so that he could look at her. See her eyes and study her with as much attention to detail as she had seemed to have given his person. Tahvo wasn't sure what to do about how he felt for a woman who was by all means a stranger, but he was bound and determined to try at least. Bound to untangle uncertainties and take care not to shatter something precious.

"You might just learn that I break a lot of glasses and rush off every time my alarm goes off." Tahvo admitted with a softness to his voice, "I cannot guarantee I will not continue to panic as I have been so far. I do not wish for you to feel as though you have to watch every step you take" Absently, he started to trace his thumb along her jawline. Just sitting there with her was soothing. Even though he had never met her before yesterday, it felt like he had sat there with her so many times before. Felt a faint pulse under his touch a lifetime ago.

That familiarity should have been comforting. Most people became hopeful if a date felt like that. Instead he was scared. Every time he became too familiar with something, things changed on him. Spot was one of those rare constants in his life and despite being a vet, he still worried every time his friend got even a little hurt or sick. The dog was absolutely spoiled by his attention and wanted for nothing. This though... he wasn't sure if Lyric would even remotely enjoy having someone fret over her well-being or need reassurance that she really was not bothered by him.

Lyric gently settled her hand on his wrist. Heart racing when her brain finally realized just how close they were sitting to each other. Suddenly she felt like she was high up on the diving board and about to jump off. Would she be able to gracefully plunge into the water or would this end more like a stinging flop?

"I don't mind. I would be happy to help you with anything that would help your anxiety not torment you as much. Glasses can always be replaced and you have animals depending on you for survival and care. I heard you've done a lot of good things for animals." She did, after all, make sure to at least try and get a feel for what people thought of him. A lot of it was very positive and frankly that made her feel more confident about coming there. "I really don't want you to be miserable, Doc-"

"You may... you may call me Tahvo if you wish." He offered softly. It wasn't often that he ever heard his name said by someone else. The fact that she was making the effort to use his name that he was most used to had been appreciated, "And if I may, Miss Helios, I would like to address you as Lyric. Also... I would very much like to grant your wish of a kiss."

Oh stars, did she really want him to kiss her right then? A tiny shy smile tugged on her lips as she murmured a soft yes. Eyes closed as they got so very close before there was suddenly an alarm going off again and he jumped. Accidentally smacking her in the nose with his chin as he jerked back to fumble with the phone and silence it. Lyric winced and rubbed at her nose.

Ow.

"Oh gods, are you alright?" Tahvo asked with a flustered look over her as he moved her hand and started to inspect her nose. It looked just a bit red but thankfully not bleeding. Who in the world let him actually agree to a date? Really?

"Yeah, I am fine." Lyric smiled to reassure him before tilting her head a bit, "So, what was that alarm for?"

"Ah..." His face got warm as he rubbed his neck, "There is a show on Animal Planet that I turn on for Spot. He really likes watching the shows about show dogs." A move to pet the dog who slowly stood up and stretched before trotting off, "I guess today he isn't as interested in it as he is making sure I don't have a heart attack."

Well, that was a very loved dog. Lyric smiled at the expectant look Spot gave them before he rose to scamper down the stairs. Finally, she stood up and offered her hand to Tahvo, "Well, let's go eat. I think I can deal with wine as a close second to tea. I bet you have a good recommendation for what goes well with chicken alfredo."

"Ah, hopefully the food isn't too cold by now. I can reheat it in the microwave if you want." Hopefully it wouldn't mess with the taste too much. At this rate, he was wondering if he would somehow give her food poisoning or something. Knowing his luck, he would. Alas, Tahvo took her hand and was startled by the ease in which she helped pull him up. He supposed gardening would require some good upper body strength. Still holding her hand, he looked down at the bandaged fingers and then her.

A deep steadying breath was taken and he tried to tell himself that he really couldn't make things much worse than they were. Except... a look down at his legs and he made a face, "I still need to change."

"I can wait for you downstairs if you want." Lyric assured him with a gentle squeeze of her hand.

"If I want?" That part hooked his attention more than any-thing. Oh, it was probably such an innocuous statement. No weight behind it, but he lifted a brow at her question-ingly. Which made Lyric consider her words before she giggled at him. Should he be insulted by the giggle?

"I mean, usually most people get dinner first *before* the pants come off." Lyric offered, covering her faux pas with teasing words instead. It was the first time she really ever had to carefully consider her words. A smile to show she didn't mean something by it, "I'll heat up our food a while. I may have ah... brought a movie for us to watch if you are interested. So if you want to forgo shoes..."

She brought a movie? Did that mean she was actually interested in spending more time with him than over a simple dinner? Before he could pick apart that entire idea, he nodded and leaned down to give her a quick chaste kiss on her cheek before drawing back, "I will try to do things in the right order. Although I do enjoy the idea of not having to wear shoes. You are welcome to forgo those as well. I promise Spot does not chew on them."

"Great!" Lyric beamed and brought his hand up to her lips and pressed a soft kiss against his knuckles before skipping off down the stairs. He stood there stunned for a moment. Hesitation held him back before he walked off to go and change into something not covered in tea. Probably a new shirt too was a good idea. Maybe if he dressed relaxed, he would feel a little more relaxed himself.

Lyric hummed as she carried both of their plates into the kitchen and placed one plate into the microwave and started letting it turn in the appliance while it heated the food. The rest of the food was still being warmed on the stove, but she didn't ever like to waste food. Something told her he had the same feelings about it. Just needed warmed up after all, and it all smelled wonderful. Which reminded her just how hungry she was.

By the time both plates had been heated, she could hear the sounds of the television being turned on and a soft voice. A smile as she carried both plates out carefully. Her hand setting the hottest food down on his end while she set the other plate down on hers. She had decided to simply put ice and water in the two glasses at the table. Something simple and he wouldn't have to worry about what sort of wine she may or may not enjoy.

When he came into the room, she felt herself almost become dizzy. He had looked good before, but now he just was breathtaking. His black hair was let loose to frame his face and the dress shirt he had on was a loose fit worn over a t shirt. The jeans he had on just tied it all in.

"I vote you spill tea on yourself more often." Lyric said softly. Seriously, holy cow! Also his hair just looked so touchable. She could tell where part of the wave was formed from pulling his hair back all of the time.

He shouldn't have felt embarrassed, but the compliment and the way she looked at him made him unsure. He should have felt flattered, "I would rather not. You would keep cutting yourself then from not being able to find the dustpan."

Brow rose and she gave a smirk, "Was that a joke?"

"Ah, perhaps." Tahvo said and then walked in a bit further and looked at the glasses. Water. Water was a good option. He probably should be drinking that anyway. He finally moved over and held out her chair for her, "I shouldn't have another alarm going off for a while. So I shouldn't be shattering anything or causing any unintended bodily harm for a bit."

"I will make sure to duck if you have the knife or fork in hand." She teased as she moved to sit down in the chair and scooted in. Despite his more comfortable style of dress, he still held himself careful and precise as he moved over to his side and finally sat down. By that point the candle's flame was within its walls of the wax giving off less light and casting dancing shadows across their faces.

Lyric stabbed a fork into her chicken and took a bite, "This is wonderful, Tahvo." The fact that she was hungry didn't make her biased. She just truly enjoyed it. After all, she sometimes could get picky and bad food wouldn't cut it if she was hungry. Besides, she had a feeling he could tell if she was lying.

Tahvo couldn't hide the shy smile pulling on the corners of his lips, "Thank you. Most people cannot go wrong with chicken alfredo. I am glad it reheated well for you."

"I think my favorite addition is the bacon you put in the sauce." Another happy sound as she ate some more. It allowed a comfortable quiet to fall over them both as they enjoyed their food. The sound of the television playing in the other room gave a soft white noise. It was a pleasant atmosphere.

It took a few moments, but Tahvo finally worked up the nerve to speak again, "So, which movie had you brought?"

"Ah, one of my favorites. Princess Bride." Lyric admitted with a soft smile. It was a pleasant movie, and she felt the cheerful tone to most of it would be perfect for a first date.

"Really?" Tahvo asked. Then he offered her a genuinely bright smile, "That is one of my favorites too."

Eyes lit up in joy, relieving Lyric of the fear that she made the wrong choice, "So, would you like to watch it after dinner then?"

Somehow, the ability of finding common ground due to a favorite film filled him with excitement that drowned out his anxiety. Lyric could see the way his expression lit up and his happiness showing through made her just as happy. His excitement was infectious.

Tahvo moved to place a hand over his chest and bowed his head. A grin pulling on his lips now as he spoke, "As you wish."

For some reason those three little words filled her face with a giddy warmth. Beaming at him, she bowed her head slightly in response, "I would make an absolutely terrible Buttercup. I'm too angry to just let someone carry me off. Bring on the electric eels. I'll take them on. The Rats of Unusual size too. They will become unusually dead." She stabbed her food with her fork to accent her words.

A long stare at the woman across the table from him before he suddenly started laughing. He had to set down his fork as he rested his hand against his forehead, "Well, then in that case I would make an awful Dread Pirate Roberts. For I really am left-handed. I can't switch off to my right one very well."

"Well, the important part would be if you can sword fight or not."

"Perhaps..."

"Wait, really?" Lyric canted her head as she studied him. Hadn't actually expected to know how to actually use a sword. Now she really wanted to see it, "So, you are a wonderful veterinarian, can cook wonderfully, and wield a sword. Any other things you can do really well?"

"Ah, I suppose you can count gardening. I landscaped everything on the property for the clinic and the house. I have always done the research for what plants were safe and which ones could benefit certain animals. Although I did discover that the catnip garden attracts quite a few stray cats and feral ones. At least there isn't an unwanted rodent problem. Although I assure you pet rats and mice are kept safe."

Tahvo felt both pleased and shy at her delight for his skills. As he described to her what other hobbies he partook in, he swore she was just going to gape at him all night. Until finally she just seemed incredibly impressed with him. It was odd having that directed at him so completely.

"Oh, that is amazing Tahvo! I thought you had a professional landscaper! I can tell you for a fact that you did a wonderful job." She rested her head on the heel of her hand as she twisted a noodle around her fork, "You have to be so busy though. I would be happy to take care of all of your gardening needs for you. Just let me know what you want cared for and what you need and I will happily do it."

That was incredibly high praise from someone who knew the nature of that kind of work. His cheeks felt warm as he smiled down at his plate while prodding at the corner of his chicken, "Thank you. That you think so makes me glad I did my research. I would very much appreciate your expertise in that manner. Your plant nursery was actually recommended to me by one of my patient's owners. What about you? What sorts of things do you, ah, enjoy?"

"Expertise is right I suppose." Lyric chuckled softly and smiled, "I have a degree in biology. I can tell you did a lot of research. All of your plants around the house are good for the cats and dogs. I would love to see what you did for the horses." At that question she made a thoughtful sound. What did she do for fun?

"A biology degree? You must really know a lot about your field then. I would be honored then to be able to contract you for regular care of my clinic's plants especially." After all, she was right about him being incredibly busy. Most of his time was spent working or preparing things for work itself.

"I do. The nursery is actually my mother's shop. We had moved here to get more space. The location definitely fits our needs. Which makes me really happy that we did. If not, I would have not met you. Although perhaps I would have met you on a walk or perhaps at the bookstore."

That little admission at the end has him looking up at her, the curves of her face just barely highlighted by the candle on the table, "The nursery did look very inviting from the outside. I would like to see the rest of it sometime. Would it be a problem if I brought Spot along with me?"

Lyric hesitated and bit her lip for a brief second, "Hm, I don't know. Let me make sure with my mother first."

Lyric set her utensils down finally after finishing her food and followed it with sipping at the water. What she wasn't saying was that despite her being an adult, the woman was still very strict and hadn't seemed to like the idea of her leaving to go on a date with someone she had just met. Understandable but... Lyric had very much wanted to see him again. So she had lied about what she was doing after work.

Tahvo nodded in understanding, "I would appreciate it. Thank you. While I do know most places allow service animals, I would prefer to play it safe if having a dog present would cause problems." He could get himself into the mindset of being a customer. Business and professional.

"Well, Spot does seem to behave really well. I don't think he will be too much of a problem." At least Lyric hoped that would be the case.

"Speaking of Spot, I should give him his treat. He has been rather well behaved." Even though he did know better. Still, he was careful about giving foods like that to him. Spot seemed to inhale everything though and continue as normal. "If you wait right here, I can bring out our dessert."

"Can we eat it while we watch the movie?" Lyric asked.

"I don't see why not. I am sure my bribery will let Spot concede his seating arrangements to us. Just be prepared if he decides your lap is a comfortable second-best option. He likes the movie too. Then you can tell me about your hobbies."

"Well, in that case I had better help clean up then." Lyric smiled. Before he could retort, she was standing up and sweeping over to him. A kiss on his cheek stunned him long enough for her to steal the stacked dishes from him and escape off into the kitchen.

Tahvo followed after her with a laugh. Between the two of them, they had cleaned the dishes, the kitchen, and put away the left-overs. Tahvo prepared a dog dish with a little of the pasta and a piece of chicken breast cut up into smaller bite sized pieces. Which Spot happily started eating as soon as it was presented to him beside his normal food.

After making sure Spot was eating, Tahvo pulled out a small tray with two ceramic bowls with lids on top of them. Lyric looked at them curiously and tried to see if she could look through the lids before she was shooed off ahead of him. He grabbed a couple of spoons and walked out after her. Tahvo watched her pull the movie out of the gift bag she brought. Despite his earlier excitement, he felt himself becoming nervous all over again.

Being across from each other at the table was one thing. Tables made barriers that gave a little comfort and security. Now he would be sitting right beside her. Oh so close and so easily touchable.

He set the dishes on the coffee table and held his hand out for the movie. Lyric handed it to him and he busied himself with setting up. It didn't take him too long and soon he was holding the remote and looking her over and then glancing towards the window, "Would you like a blanket?"

Lyric nodded and before she could accompany her answer with a voice, she was handed the remote and watched him leave. It was hard not to peek at the waiting dessert, but he had mentioned it was a surprise. So, despite her curiosity, she waited.

Plus, the way he was moving around told her that he was starting to become anxious again. There was no way she was going to purposefully exasperate anything. She was determined to take great care in letting him do things at his own pace.

It didn't take long for him to return with a large coppery fleece blanket. An incredibly soft one by the feel of it. She closed her eyes as he draped it around her shoulders. The massive blanket about drowned her and she looked down at her feet. Rather the pooling blanket that covered her feet.

"I think there is enough blanket here for the two of us."

"I am tall, so I tend to get a lot of massive blankets to accommodate legs and my pet horse." Tahvo admitted with a smirk. He motioned for her to sit down and proceeded to peel the lids off the desserts and held one out to her with the spoon sticking out of it from the side. He watched her peer into the dish while she carefully held it in her hand.

"What is it?" She dipped her pinky into the vanilla pudding and stuck it into her mouth. A tiny action that made him hesitate before clearing his throat and carefully sitting beside the blanket swamped woman.

"Pomegranate jelly with pudding and some pomegranate arils on top." He replied with a smile as he watched her poke at one of the seeds.

"It looks lovely."

"Yes. The seeds and the fruit around them are all edible. I promise it is safe." He felt himself smile as she looked hesitantly at it. Finally, he spooned up a small bite that had the jelly, vanilla, and at least a couple seeds and he held it out to her. He hadn't even thought about what he was doing until he saw her blinking at the offered spoon and hesitantly closing her mouth around it. He watched her work through the tastes of the more bitter fruit and jelly blended with the far creamier sweeter pudding. It was a flavor he found he enjoyed. Even if getting the arils out of the pomegranate was always a mildly annoying task.

Lyric considered her dessert for a moment and then scooped up some with her spoon and held it out to him in return, "Oh I know. I like it. You really *are* good at making food. I would love if you could teach me some of your recipes. Maybe I can share some of mine with you or next time we do this, we can make dinner together."

Next time? Next time. Would there be a next time? His lips parted as though trying to work out a response before he nodded silently. The fear of saying something to ruin it thrummed in him. The fact he commented about the safety of *pomegranate* to someone who worked with plants made him want to hit his head against a wall. Instead of speaking, he very delicately took the bite off her spoon and settled down. At least he tried to before suddenly she was moving around all too much and he found the blanket draped around his shoulders and her body pressed against the side of his.

She was incredibly warm against him. The large plush sofa made it all the more comfortable and he watched her pull her legs up as she relaxed against him. The movie started and it took him a few moments to look away from her and to relax into the sofa. In silence he ate, though with her leaning against his arm, it was a touch difficult. Finally, he gave up and took a few much larger bites of the small dessert before setting the dish on the table and leaning back to curl his arm around her shoulders so that she fit comfortably under his arm. An act he thought nothing of until he did it.

It was eerie how familiar this felt and more so how perfect she seemed to fit under his arm. He held his breath until she snuggled more and finished her own dessert. Every so often, he could hear her quoting the movie. On some occasions, he joined in with her and was rewarded with the most brilliant sounding laughter.

By the end, they were both quoting it. Speaking along with the movie. They were laughing and smiling together so easily. Lyric had taken to intertwining her hand with the hand of the arm wrapped around her and her head resting slightly against his chest. Spot had come out partway through and was laying on the floor against his legs. Tahvo Melanthios felt content. For the first time in a long time he realized that before he met Lyric Helios, he had been missing something important. A heart to beat beside his.

3

Lyric had eventually dozed off against him after he had escaped only once during the movie to feed the puppies for the last time in the night. It was not something Tahvo had expected at all. In fact, he was actually rather unsure of how to respond to her sleeping there.

Spot made it harder by sleeping on his legs, making it near impossible to get up without startling anyone else. In the end, Tahvo had given up and tried to get some rest himself. After all, he did have to work tomorrow. He imagined she did too. A shift to get a little more comfortable and he soon discovered himself falling into a deep sleep.

It was on rare occasions that he got dreams that made no sense. Like pictures of flitting memories, but nothing was ever in order. Nothing seemed to fit together at all. He just knew that most of it was cold and miserable. If those really were memories of some sort of past life, he could have done without recalling those.

These dreams that came instead were warmer. While there was that biting cold, there was a smile that brought warmth.

Laughter that rang forever in his ears when he heard it, and haunted him with a longing when he woke and the source was not there. A hand intertwined with his. Painful goodbyes and passionate greetings. A name he had never heard before, but he felt like it should have been his; Hades.

The other name sounded so much sweeter to him. A name that passed on a whisper of lips. Hands running along the skin. Fingers tangled in hair. Tahvo reached out for the name; Persephone. It was a name that inspired warmth and adoration. Tahvo didn't understand why, but it made him feel something akin to the comfort and familiarity that Lyric did at that moment. Perhaps he was just going insane from all of that work he was doing.

Then he saw the briefest glimpse of an ornate box before he woke up to his phone going off. Lyric stretched lazily before she looked up at him. He groggily opened his eyes to see the sunlight slowly drifting through the windows. A yawn as Tahvo pulled his phone out and dismissed the alarm. He had slept with Lyric there the whole night. He didn't want to get up from that spot. Not with the way they had shifted to where he was laying back across the length of the sofa and her slightly pulled onto his chest and nestled between his legs.

His hand hesitated before he gently smoothed his fingers over her hair and helped brush it out of her face, "Sorry I hadn't woken you up. Between you and Spot, I would have felt terrible for disturbing you both from such a peaceful sleep."

"Hm?" Lyric blinked and it took her a few good moments to realize where she was at and who she was with. Also the fact that dawn was there escaped her until the moment she peered at the window that showed a dusky grey outside. "What time is it?"

"About six in the morning." He responded with a lazy drawl. If he wanted, he could have so easily fallen asleep with listening to her tired voice while playing with that soft hair. At least until he felt her go stiff in his arms and she shot up from the sofa so quickly that she tumbled to the floor. That action woke him up fast when her elbow accidentally jabbed his ribs in her effort to get up. Spot barely managed to dodge the feet and falling woman. Tahvo tried to roll over to help her up, and instead fell himself.

"I'm late! I was supposed to be there an hour ago! Shit shit shit! Mom is going to kill me." Lyric started to go on a search for her shoes. Eyes wide as she went on her hunt.

Slowly, Tahvo stood up slowly after untangling himself from the blanket and walked towards the door where he had put her shoes last night and held them out to her. A bleary rub of his eyes and he yawned, "Let me get my shoes on and I can drive you there."

"Oh no, Tahvo, I can-"

"It's alright. I can even explain to her that it was my fault you didn't wake up on time. I should have made sure you got home last night." He assured her before hesitating for a moment then gently cupping her face and kissing her nose. It was such a familiar little act that possessed him. He drew back and smiled hopefully to her, "Just wait, please?"

"Okay." Lyric said softly and blinked as she watched him balance on one long leg as he works to pull his first shoe on and then another. Rather, they looked like biker boots. It was something rather mesmerizing to watch him pull a leather jacket off a hook and pull it on. Though she was surprised when he held out an older more worn jacket towards her.

"You are going to need this." He said. Waiting for her to finished getting dressed, he looked over her, "Be right back, Spot. Keep an eye on the pups." A sleepy woof was his response before the large dog stretched and did a lazy walk towards the steps and climbing them to look over the pups. Tahvo went do the door off to the right of the stairs and opened it to show a garage. One bay with a car in it and another with a motorcycle.

Picking up the helmet, he frowned when he realized he only had one. Turning towards Lyric, he held it out to her, "You should wear this."

"I can walk, it really isn't that far away." Lyric insisted. Finally she relented and took the helmet at his insistent look. Guilt tugged at her as he ran his fingers through his hair and pulled it up and back and tied it off at the nape of his neck. She didn't want him to put himself in danger over her being late.She watched as he pulled the keys out of his jacket pocket and approach the copper and black motorcycle. It was one of the kinds you sat up on instead of forward. Not a sporty thing so much as something to relax and drive with.

"Yes, but that will take you at least an hour. On this, it will take perhaps ten minutes." Tahvo told her and motioned for her to come over while he checked it over. Then he opened the garage door, "The sooner you get there, the less trouble you will be in. I would be happy to keep you from getting into trouble, Lyric. Please allow me to help."

"Well..." When he said please like that, it was hard to say no, "Okay. Thank you, Tahvo." She climbed onto the back of the motorcycle after he did. Pulling on the helmet, she made sure it fit alright before wrapping her arms around his waist. With it on, the sounds were muffled as the bike roared to life and he pulled out. A push of a button mounted to the bike and the garage door closed behind them as he drove down his path and turned off into the street.

He was right, the trip really was faster this way. Lyric kept her arms wrapped around his waist. It wasn't often that she got to be on a motorcycle. Much less with someone she enjoyed being with. After all, she owned a safe little green Volkswagen bug. Not that she minded this form of transportation at all, this was fun. Tahvo made her feel nice and safe as he coasted to a stop in front of her store. The ride had been over all too quick and she felt a slight daze at the fact that one moment she had been at his house and what felt like just a few minutes later she was there. Especially after having walked there from work the night before. Lyric frankly hated her car. It was embarrassingly noisy for such a small machine.

Then again, she realized that perhaps the reason she wanted to walk was to delay having to face her mother. Lyric wasn't ready to climb off the bike as they pulled in front of the shop. Instead she allowed him to gently peel her arms from around his waist. He managed to swing his legs off without making her fall. She discovered her legs were a little too wobbly for standing and soon he scooped her up and gently set her down on the ground. She fumbled for a moment and pulled the helmet off once she felt like the ground was steady beneath her feet.

"We really need to do that again. That was too short of a ride!" She pouted.

Tahvo laughed and smoothed her hair as best he could. A nervous habit she assumed given he looked nearly apologetic over his actions, "We'll need to get you a better jacket and helmet next time. Perhaps..." He hedged, "on our next date."

"A next date? So you really want to do this again?" The hopeful grin made her face glow. She lifted up a hand to brush her fingers against his windblown cheeks, "I'm game to go again whenever you are."

"Good, although…" he looked her over, studying the way she looked in his old jacket. His fingers ran along the collar of it, "I like the way my old jacket looks on you. If you would like to keep it, I would be very pleased."

"Well, it is a very comfortable jacket. I would also love to go out again this weekend after work. I can wear it then too." Lyric said. A giddy warmth spilled through her.

"As you wish, Princess Lyric." He bowed to her dramatically and then studied her for a brief moment before stepping forward. One knuckle gently hooked under her chin to tilt her head up a little more towards him, "So Princess, may I kiss you?"

"Hmm, I don't know. It might not be appropriate for a pirate to *request* a kiss from a princess. I thought they stole those." She whispered her response. He was so close to her right now. In all honestly, the morning breath didn't even remotely bother her in that moment.

"While it is certainly appropriate for a Pirate to steal one, for you I would make this exception. For I think it is you who stole away my very mind so that you occupy my thoughts." He mused in response. Words just as quiet. Tahvo was just about to close the distance when a shrill voice screamed Lyric's name. He frowned when Lyric drew back with a jerk and started cursing.

"Lyric Helios!" The woman, Dinara, yelled as she approached the pair with rushed steps, "You're late!" Then a look at the jean clad male with windblown hair, "And who the hell is this?!"

A sudden protective urge surged up within Tahvo and he placed himself a step in front of Lyric to defend her. The first thing he noted about the tall willowy woman was the golden-brown eyes. Silver streaked blonde hair was pulled back tight against her head in a bun, making her look far more severe. Her skin was a dark tan from being outside all of the time, and it simply added to the aging lines at her eyes and on her face.

"I am Doctor Melanthios." He responded evenly. Only very few people knew his first name, "I am the reason that she is late. I had let her sleep in. Had I been aware of the hour she should have been here, I would have woken her up."

That did nothing to soothe the woman's fury. Instead she just glared past him and to her daughter, "So, you just slept with a man you just met? Does him being a doctor make it acceptable?" She reached out to grab at her daughter and sneered when Tahvo blocked her with his own arm, "Move out of the way, *Doctor*, and stay away from my daughter."

Tahvo was about to say something before he felt Lyric's hand on his arm, "It's okay." She told him softly and then steps around him to frown at her mother,

"I did nothing more than actually *sleep*, Mom. Besides, I am an adult, I am old enough to do whatever I want with

whomever I want. Comes with that whole bodily autono-
my I told you about."

"Get inside, Lyric, and go change into something that
doesn't make you lo-"

"Mom! Would you just stop?!" Lyric shouted and angrily
started to stalk off to the store before forgetting herself and
spinning on heel and marching back to Tahvo.

Her expression softened as she held his helmet out to him,
"Here. Thank you very much for dinner and letting me get
a good night's rest."

The soft dejected voice made Tahvo's heart clench. The
remnants of his dreams whispered of the painful goodbyes
the Hades in his head felt every time with his Persephone.
Thinking of that, he very carefully took the helmet from
her. As he did so with one hand, he found himself cupping
the back of her head with his other one. Fingers sinking
into soft colorful hair as he pressed his lips against hers.
A soft and thorough kiss as he felt her respond to him in
kind. When he drew back, he felt dizzy.

"Thank you for your delightful company. I look forward to
this weekend, Princess."

His voice was a bare whisper and he tried very hard to
ignore the fuming woman that could kill with just a look.
Honestly, Tahvo wasn't sure what came over him at that
moment. Though he wasn't about to regret it when Lyric

brightened after being screeched at for her choices, "If you need anything, Miss Helios, you have my number."

Lyric worked on relearning how to breathe properly when her heart wanted to leap right out of her chest. Without her realizing, her hand had gone to settle on his chest when they had kissed. His heart pounded away just as insanely hard as her own did, "Of course my pirate. You have mine as well for the same reasons. See you this weekend."

Tahvo nodded, relieved that she didn't seem upset with him kissing her somewhat unexpectedly. Reluctantly, he drew back and pulled his helmet on. The tall male swung his leg over his bike and peeled off with a short squeal of his tires.

Lyric watched him until he vanished down a turn. Fingers touching against her lips before she broke into a bright smile. That all too sunny smile was directed towards her mother before she skipped off right to the shop.

Dinara on the other hand, scowled. Anger filled her with every step she took to follow after her daughter. As soon as they made it to the back of the shop, she reached out almost lightning fast and snatched Lyric's arm with her own hand.

"I told you yesterday not to go out! You don't need to be traipsing off with every person that happens to have two legs, a smile, and a working phone number like your father had!"

"I also told you that I am an adult. My romantic life is absolutely none of your business." Lyric pulled her arm away roughly and rubbed it. Gods, her mother could be so overbearing. As time went on, things got worse and her mother grew more physical in her anger. Lyric wasn't entirely sure yet as to why she put up with it at all.

"It most certainly is my business who your flavor of the week is when your last boy toy set my shop on fire." Dinara snapped.

"He wasn't my boy toy! He was a stalker! One who didn't understand the word no! It isn't my fault he took offense to me agreeing to date a girl when I kept refusing him!"

"If you didn't just go on dates whenever it suited your whim, maybe he wouldn't have thought you easy enough to ask you out and expect you to say yes in the first place." There was an indelicate snort , "I swear child, you are nothing but trouble. If you would just listen to me-"

"I am not easy!" Lyric snapped. She shook her head in the building anger that rose to drown the panic of memories. Her good mood was dwindling, "Dates are meant to let you get to know someone to see if you want to do anything more with them other than have a coffee together. It isn't any of your business if I actually sleep with them or not. Oh if only you kne-"

"Enough! I am tired of your attitude! It is your fault we are out here! Take off that hideous thing now!" A gesture towards the back of the shop, "And get to work! You have several orders to fill and someone wants to make a contract for landscaping their office property."

Lyric gave her a look that said she wanted to say so many things that would probably lead to her being slapped. Instead, she adjusted her jacket and marched back towards her personal office where she kept her work clothes.

"Just leave the orders and the number of the business on the table. I happen to have another contract I am setting up with anyway. The Elysian Fields needs some work done."

"It is already on your desk. You would have known that if you would have been here on time." Her mother said tersely. A turn around to go back out to the shop. The phone started ringing and she added, "Make yourself useful and pick up the phone. It's probably another order."

Lyric watched her mother leave and sighed as she went back to her office. She finally picked up the phone and her tone was absent as she saw herself in the mirror. His coat was really too large on her, but she loved it. It smelled of him, "Seraphic Plant Nursery, this is Lyric speaking."

"Yes, this is Doctor Melanthios from the Elysian Fields Clinic and Shelter. I had wanted to inquire about landscaping maintenance for my business. I was told that this would be the number to call." His voice sounded all business like, but she could hear the amusement of trying to keep his tone professional and level. It made Lyric smile. Hearing his voice immediately made her feel worlds better.

"Well, hello Doctor Melanthios. I would be more than happy to assist you. Are you interested in a regularly scheduled maintenance or a one-time visit just to get everything into shape?" Lyric asked as she kicked her door shut. She leaned against her desk and a smile pulled hard on her lips. She swore her heart was racing again and she could feel his kiss that lingered.

She must have said something amusing as she heard him shift and chuckle. That professionalism was slipping, "I think something of a long-term arrangement would be far more beneficial for us, Miss Lyric."

The way her name rolled off his tongue made her think back to the kiss again and she shuddered, "I believe that we can arrange something in that manner. What sort of work were you looking to have done?"

"Just want to ensure that the layout is beneficial to the needs of the animals I care for in the clinic. Weeding, repotting, and perhaps unforeseen needs for some of the other plant life. I do have a list of what grows for each area."

"Excellent. I think all I would need to do is do an initial visit to see what I have to work with and give you a quote. I have some appointments earlier in the day, but after my last one, I can squeeze you in about four-thirty." She couldn't help but smile as she leaned over and he confirmed the time. A scribble of the name of the clinic in her book after looking at the other things she needed to do.

"I look forward to meeting you, Miss Lyric. When you come, just speak to Mr. Cheroni and ask for me. He will know I am waiting for you." He was smiling and it showed in his voice.

"See you then, thank you for choosing us, Doctor Melan-thios."

"Quite welcome, Miss Lyric. Have a wonderful day."

"I already am." She promised and found herself making a soft kissing sound goodbye on the phone before hanging up and staring at it. Had he inferred that they should have a steady relationship on the phone? It sure sounded like there was a double meaning behind those words. Not only that, but did she just hang up from him with a goodbye kiss? It was a total accident but... she didn't regret it.

Oh yes, Lyric knew she was absolutely lost. A very sure part of her told her that Tahvo was worth every broken heart she had ever gotten. Every nightmare she had ever woken from, and certainly would be worth the absolute fear she had from losing the last shop while she was in it. A shudder at the memory of fire before she shoved the thought away and quickly changed into her overalls and a button-up shirt. Hair pulled back tightly and a cap pulled on before she started to move through the shop to load the flowers already sorted into her car. She had pulled the leather jacket on and the scent of him lingering on it kept her company.

Lyric spent the rest of the day driving around new orders, using her GPS to figure out where to go. In a new area, that was even more important than before. It gave her a chance to relearn everything. The first meeting about a contract was actually an easy one. They wanted a little bit of something around the front of the local elementary school. So she scheduled something for the next day. Busy work to keep her away from the shop.

As it neared the end of her day as she pulled up her little car into the clinic parking and looked at her clipboard. A flipping of papers of the day's receipts and the first contract. A little more shuffling and she pulled the newest contract up to the top. The business' name carefully written at the top and she climbed out of her car and tucked her clip board under her arm. There was a thorough study as she approached the front of the clinic, a critical eye on the landscape itself. It was serene and welcoming, splashes of colors and greens to ease away the daunting feeling most would feel when approaching any unknown clinic. Lyric finally stepped inside and looked about at the currently quiet waiting room before looking at the male scribbling notes at his desk. Eyes drew up and they studied each other for a long moment.

Mr. Cheroni looked familiar somehow, but she couldn't place it. Instead of dwelling on that, she smiled and approached, "Hello, I am looking for Doctor Melanthios. He said he would be expecting me about now. I am Lyric Helios from the Seraphic Plant Nursery."

It felt... unnerving for the man to look over her as though accessing her very soul before he nodded and pressed the button on the phone at the desk.

"Doctor Melanthios, there is a Miss Helios here to see you." Very careful and deliberate with every word as to not be misunderstood.

A long moment of silence and then a voice responded, "Please escort her back to my office."

James nodded at the phone as though his nod could be heard before straightening and motioning for her to follow him. He walked in silence and Lyric felt slightly unnerved as she followed. Although the hallway was painted as something warm and sunny to combat it. The floors were a grass green tile which worked with the bases of the walls painted like grass and flowering fields. The walls looked like distant mountains and blue skies and sunsets. The walk behind the eerily silent man went from uncomfortable to relaxing as though the very atmosphere of the place brought her peace. She could definitely see why Tahvo could be a very popular vet.

When they stopped walking, James pointed to the door, "Knock here." He then walked back down the hall, leaving Lyric to stand in front of the door. Suddenly, she felt hesitant. After a deep breath she finally raised her hand

and knocked on the door. There was suddenly a lot of scrambling sounds on the other side of the door and a lot of barking. She could hear the sounds of Tahvo's voice telling the dogs to settle down and a loud fetch before thunderous feet became quiet and he opened the door.

Lyric looked up to see glasses framing Tahvo's eyes and his dark hair pulled back. A nice clean dress shirt and slacks completed the look. A fair difference from his jeans and leather of that morning. They smiled at each other when he ushered her in. It gave her a chance to look around the office. The one wall was a large sliding glass doors that led out into the dog run where the pack of dogs were all running around and playing. Spot was out there with them, running around with a large tug-of-war rope and leading the others on a grand chase. Someone was outside with them, keeping an eye on them to ensure they all behaved.

"Aww, he is your helper!"

That made Tahvo laugh then smiled at her, "Ah yes, he likes to be the pack leader and run them around. Gives them all exercise." He moved over to his desk and leaned over it, scratching something down in pen, "I apologize if my... forward behavior caused you any trouble today."

He tried not to look at her when he apologized. In all honesty he didn't know what drove him to do that. He wondered if the dreams he had before pushed him to do anything. Given his luck, if he told her about the dreams, she would just think he was delusional.

"What do you-" Lyric blinked then her brain clicked, "Oh! That! Nah, don't worry about it. Mom is always pretty grumpy about everything." Was he really so worried about it? Then she gave a playful smile, "I am just glad I finally got the kiss I asked for. We seemed to have had quite a time of it trying to get just one kiss."

"Ah, well…" He cleared his throat a little and looked towards the glass doors and then straightened, "May I give you a proper tour of the grounds, Miss Helios?" An attempt at professionalism, but he still stole a look towards her. The way his eyes trailed over her face told Lyric that he might have been considering another kiss.

Given how quickly he changed topics, Lyric figured professionalism was for the best and nodded. It was better to drop the current conversation for when he was more at ease anyway. Something told her that kissing people to aggravate their parents was not a common practice for him. Although it did prove to her that there was quite a bit of mischief hiding under that anxious demeanor. Lyric nodded and stepped outside ahead of him and looked at the dog run itself. A smile shone brightly at the way the plants were laid out along the fences. A careful attention to detail as to which ones were safe or not. It looked well loved, but she certainly could see where just a few weeds were making their way into the dog garden.

She let him lead her along through the property. She got to see where all of the cats lazed about and where the rabbits grazed. The horses had to be one of her favorite parts as he introduced her to them all and pointed out the few that were specifically his. Her favorite part was his off-handed comment that it would be nice to have someone with him to help give the horses a run. Riding certainly was something she wanted to learn how to do.

His tour took her to the reptile part of the clinic where all manner of snakes, lizards, and even a lone crocodile spent their time. There were so many animals there and she had to wonder how he cared for them all. At least until he explained that Mr. Cheroni and a few other trusted vet techs were employed to assist him. After all, Tahvo was but one person and plenty of animals needed his attention. They rounded back to the office and she watched as he ushered the sprawling dogs to come inside as the sun set. Lyric blinked as Spot trotted over with a pretty spotted long haired dog who sniffed at her shoes and wagged its tail.

Very slowly, Lyric knelt down and held her hand out to the dog and watched as it sniffed at her hand for a long moment. The dog continued to snuffling at it before licking her fingers. Lyric giggled and scratched the mid-sized dog behind the ear, "This dog is so soft! The spots are so cute too." She watched the dog promptly sit down as though having chosen this as a preferable place to be instead of the kennel. A check of the collar and she blinked and smiled at it, "Asteri. That is such a pretty name!"

"She is usually pretty shy." Tahvo mused and then a thought struck him as he knelt down too and held his hand out for the long-haired dog, "I do believe you seem to have that effect on people. She is a bit older so I haven't found her a home quite yet." The long-haired dog was white with a smattering of black spots all over her fur. A thoughtful sound, "If you would like, I could bring her over to my house and the next time you visit, you could have more time to acquaint yourself with her. In case you would perhaps like to keep her."

"I would love that, Tahvo! Oops, I mean Doctor Melanthios." Lyric gave an apologetic look. She always wanted a pet. During the move, she at least had managed to get her own place. It was still only a door or two down from her mother's place, but it would allow her to get a pet. No worries about complaints over dog hair getting on the furniture, "Is she good with cats?"

A smile as she caught herself and Tahvo nodded, "So far she doesn't seem to have a problem with them. I would certainly suggest an older cat who already has an even temperament and is used to dogs. Most of the ones here are by necessity, but it would be good to make sure whatever cat you have will be agreeable with Asteri."

"Ah, not have so much as want. I want a cat too sometime. I love both." Lyric smiled as she pet the happy dog and watched her prop her front paws on her knee. It filled her with a serene warmth, "Meanwhile, we should pick a day for me to come here and work on the gardens here."

"Well, I do hold Saturday hours in the morning. Depending on your allowed timeframe, there is an option to work on that until you do have to get off of work. It would make it easier to take one on a date. Perhaps for the horses or motorcycles..." Words trailed off as he hoped she would take to the idea. A nervous look away as he pet Spot. Was he doing all of this right? When was his last real relationship?

Lyric let the idea sink in and her smile almost seemed devilish. It certainly would work out well for her. Complete her work first and then spend some time with him until she had to go home, "Movies would be an excellent pastime too. As well as dinner around that time. Saturdays it is then. About five o'clock I would be able to do some work until seven. That should let you have some time to prepare for whatever fun activities you have planned, right? The perfect *long-term arrangement.*"

Weekly dates. She agreed to possible weekly dates after work for them both. Tahvo finally looked at her and smiled softly, "As you wish." He bowed his head with a smile and then stood, "Unfortunately, I imagine you have to get back. Your mother probably would not take kindly to me stealing all of your time for a second day in a row."

"No," Lyric sighed softly, "She'd probably overreact and accuse you of abduction or something." She shook her head and she lifted up her clipboard, "I do need to fill this out though. Although... perhaps if we put Mr. Cheroni's name in there as the contact, then my mother may not become nosey about dates."

That made him chuckle a little and he nodded, "I was about to suggest that anyway. I do not generally feel comfortable speaking on the phone. I rarely enjoy repeating myself. It is worse when signal on a phone is spotty at best. He is far better at it."

There was a moment of hesitation before offering his hand to her and helping her stand up. His lips came to caress her knuckles when she stood up fully. He didn't want to say goodbye again. Perhaps space for the next few days would be good for them.

That, or it would end up being a near absolute torture for them both.

Tahvo certainly hoped it would just be a mere space between them and not keep him from focusing. Distraction could be terrible. She wasn't consuming his every thought at least. Though he found he very much wanted to lift her up and set her on his desk so that he can kiss her more easily and keep her there for just a bit longer. Instead he restrained himself. The kiss he gave had pushed enough boundaries. Patience would be his friend, even if it felt like some sort of self-inflicted punishment.

"I will walk you out to your car. I will see you on Saturday then, Miss Helios." His voice reigned in to disguise the want he felt. That kiss he had stolen earlier had his head buzzing with ideas of what more he could do with that soft mouth of hers. What he could do to her with his own.

"I look forward to my first day here, Doctor Melanthios. I will call you during the week to let you know what my fee will be once I compile a list of supplies I will be bringing with me." She started to scribble something down and then as she filled out the paperwork. She signed one bit and then marked one part.

"We will have Mr Cheroni sign after we have agreed on price and he will be the main contact. First payment will likely be a little more given I will be bringing plants in to help fill the garden out."

"Thank you, I am sure you will do a great job giving the clinic and all of the occupants exactly what they need." Tahvo moved to the door to his office and gave a short whistle at Spot and Asteri, "You two sit and stay. I will be right back." He then let Lyric out into the hallway and walked with her through the building. They stopped with Mr. Cheroni and explained the paper work. Then Tahvo let her out to the parking lot.

The sun was already setting and he knew he needed to get home to the puppies and cat he was caring for. He had run back and forth between the clinic and house all day to help feed them. For now they were sleeping, but he knew soon would be feeding time again.

Lyric stopped beside her little safe car and looked up at Tahvo. She didn't want to leave. It felt like somehow she had done it thousands of times before. Even though she knew she would see him again in just a few days. Lyric looked up at him and knew, while it was wholly unprofessional, she wanted to kiss him.

Well, screw professional! Lyric went up onto her toes and threw her arms around his neck to get that bit of height needed to press her lips against his. Her cap fell off and she could feel him snatch it out of the air while his other was tucked against the small of her back.

He kissed her back softly, making a needy sound as he gently pinned her against the side of her car so he could set the cap down on the roof. With the newly freed hand, Tahvo tangled that hand into her hair and deepened the kiss. He wasn't sure what about her made him forget himself and that careful self-control, but it was hard to worry about that when she was responding in kind.

When they both came up for air, he laughed softly, "This must be a really good dream."

How else could he have possibly even mustered up the nerve to kiss her like that? Hell, they were both dressed for work and he had her pinned against her car like they were both a couple of love sick hormonal teenagers. It was a good thing they didn't start taking each other's clothes off.

"If this is a dream, then I hope the alarm doesn't go off." Lyric responded with a giggle and a stolen kiss against his jaw. If this was a dream, he was the best damn dream she had ever had. Eyes closed as she snuggled against him, "I honestly have no desire to go back to the shop or go back home right now."

"Why do you go back?" He asked softly. Holding her close to him, he played idly with her hair. Did her mother really have so much say over the decisions of the woman he currently held?

There was a bitter smile, "Student loans are a bitch and at the time I was too young to get them as an independent student. I had been denied. So the Bank of Mom had to help put me through college. She refused to pay for anything but the very best. I am still paying her back for all of my tuition that she demands I compensate her for. The agreement came with rules that she actually made into a legal document. Notarized and all."

Which she had a lot more leeway before the shop had been set on fire. Now she was also roped into having to help pay for the new shop on top of her loans. Lyric didn't generally keep much money for herself in an effort to pay it off faster. At the time, Lyric had figured that she would get an excellent job in her field, pay off the loans quickly and be able to finally find her own way. Now she was ten years out and much further away from her goal. At least it didn't come with interest. Yet.

Tahvo frowned, "That is not a healthy relationship with anyone's mother. What happens if you break her so called rules of agreement?"

"It isn't as though I am not aware of that, Tahvo. She has the ability and right to seize all of my assets according to the fine print. Not like I have very much that is mine. I try to pay her back as much as I can every time I have money. I refuse to live with her again. One room apartments are not all that horrible." She forced a sunny smile despite realizing that he was staring at her like she sprouted a second head.

Tahvo had a sinking feeling and spoke again, "And if she dislikes whomever you are dating?"

"Ah well…" Lyric frowned a little. Very few dates ever made it past the first one. It was an absolutely shitty situation, "That one is more complicated." She loosened her arms around his neck and looked away. A lot of good her degree did for her when she was stuck in such a situation. Lyric should have known better back then, but she had been so much more focused on getting a degree in the field she enjoyed and getting the hell out. Now she was trapped.

"I should get going. I need to file this paperwork." Her voice soft as she felt him hesitate and then gently set her down, "I will see you Saturday, Doctor Melanthios. I think… it may be better for your sake if we keep our relationship professional. I did very much enjoy our date, but I would hate to impose." He was sweet and had such a gentle heart, Lyric couldn't stand doing that to him. Hell, she couldn't bear to look up at him.

Tahvo stared a moment before he nodded numbly and stepped back. With years of practice he schooled his expression as he straightened his back. She wouldn't even look up at him, "As you wish. I apologize for my continued forwardness. I hope that any trouble you have gotten into because of me does not cause you any lasting harm. Have a good evening, Miss Helios."

Before she could say much more, she watched him give a short bow and turn around. His gait was stiff, but he managed to hold his head high somehow. Though gods only knew how he felt. Lyric felt her throat get tight and eyes burned as she glared at her car and nearly wished she could just rip the door off the hinges. Another glare spared at the clipboard and she threw it into the back seat and drove off.

It was a short drive and she barely remembered to lock her car as she grabbed the clipboard and marched into the shop from the side door. Anger made it easier to ignore her mother as she stalked back to her office and slammed the door. She leaned against the door and sagged. Tears escaped down her cheeks. Lyric felt like such an idiot. She knew her mother would never have approved of her ever dating anyone ever again. So why had she gone and asked for Tahvo out on a date in the first place? He was probably better off without the sort of trouble she could bring. So why did her chest hurt so much as though she just ripped something out of her? After all, she had only met him a couple of days ago. Only had one date and shared but two kisses.

Lyric had to wonder if it would hurt this much when she saw him again in a few days. That thought clawed at her head as she moved to her chair and plopped down. A turn of her chair to her printer as she turned it on and then her computer. In silence she worked on scanning the documents in and putting them in the appropriate folder. As she worked, she heard the phone ring. After a couple trills, she finally lifted the phone up to her ear and gave her standard greeting. The voice she heard on the other side made her blood go cold.

"Hello, Lyric."

4

Lyric slammed the phone down and stared at it. When the phone started ringing again, she panicked and unplugged it. She shoved it off of her desk with a loud crash. Could still hear the phones in the rest of the nursery ringing. She refused to answer it. Her body trembled and she shakily finished scanning the papers. Her eyes went to the little business card of Tahvo's on her desk and she reached for it before drawing her hand back. No. She wasn't going to involve him in this.

Instead, she finished up her work and changed out of her uniform and into her clothes from earlier. Numbly she pulled Tahvo's coat on and tugged it tightly around her. It made her feel a little better, but now there was an added pain. Lyric suddenly wanted to call him and tell him that she really was scared. Instead, she changed her hold to have her keys protrude from between her fingers of her clenched hand and left her office and locked the door to it before going out the side door. For the pure reason keeping herself from feeling trapped, she started walking down the sidewalk to the little apartment complex she lived in.

It at least was a short walk. A whole ten minutes and she was already at the complex. She started to use her keycard to get into the main door as she heard feet behind her. With her thoughts racing, she tried to furiously ignore it before something slammed the door with a loud thump. It made Lyric jump and spin around to stare at an all too familiar face. Intense grey-blues leered at her and in limited light his normally brown hair looked black. He had a black jacket on and his breath smelled strongly of alcohol. Her back pressed hard against the door, fingers curling tightly around her keys as she stared up at him. Swallowing her fear as best she could, she tried to put a hand on his chest to push him back. It failed given there was such limited space to move he was leaning towards her.

"I didn't know you knew my brother so *intimately*, Lyric. You should have told me." He seemed so very amused, but the tone was off. That sickening tone of being offended exactly like the last time...

"Your brother? I don-" Oh gods. Oh gods he was going to hurt someone. He was going to hurt *her*.

"Don't try lying to me. You looked awfully familiar with him today at your shop." His sickly sweet smile turned into a bored frown. He watched her freeze and stare up at him.

"Oh, you didn't know Tahvo was my brother? Yeah, I guess he is too embarrassed to talk about his brother. Thinks he is better than the rest of us."

Lyric felt her heart drop into her stomach and she shook her head, "I only just met him. We're not-" They weren't dating. Not really. She had made sure to break that off quickly. Not that Stephen cared in any sense of the word. She had went on one tiny date with someone last time and despite it being an innocent little thing, he had set the old shop on fire with her inside of it.

Her voice was small, "Please, Stephen. Don't bother him. We aren't... I just... I just want to be left alone."

"Sure you aren't, that's why you were kissing on him at his clinic, right?" He smiled slowly as he watched her start to panic before he lifted up a hand to touch her cheek, "Save yourself the trouble and date a real man. He can't do anything but cower in a corner and whimper. Even after going through so much trouble to get what he wants, he can't even fight for it now. Coward."

Despite fear for herself, the way he spoke about Tahvo had lit a spark. Lyric glared at him, "He is a better man than you will ever be. You are just a selfish asshole. Back off! Don't you *dare* bother Tahvo!" She tried to shove him away again, hands hitting his chest with as much force as she could muster in such a small space. Making sure her keys dug in when she did so.

This time, he reacted by using his other hand to slam her arm against the door. Pain shot through her wrist as she screamed. In a panic fueled by the need to escape, she raised her foot enough to kick hard at his knee. The strike resulted in a satisfying popping sound and him swearing loudly as he crumbled. Instead of turning to try and open her door, Lyric jumped over him and bolted down the street as hard and as fast as possible. He screamed things at her that she couldn't understand in her panic. She tried to right her pain scrambled brain. Clawing at any semblance of coherent thought as to where she was supposed to go. How did he find out where she lived?

A car came to a screeching stop along the street as she ran. She barely noticed the blue vehicle did a u-turn and drove along side of her. Windows opened as the driver leaned over. It was Mr. Cheroni and he looked concerned, "Miss Helios, is something the matter?"

Suddenly being addressed by name had a strangled sound escaping her and she had to clutch her chest as she froze in place and stared at the man in the car. "I..." Lyric was panting and she tried to find the air to form words. The woman looked behind her, half expecting Stephen to just be looming behind her. Eyes were wide with darting looks going between the man in the car and behind her.

Then she gave up trying to decide if this was safe and nodded wordlessly. At least it was someone she knew. Well, knew of. When she heard the click of doors unlocking, tears welled up in her eyes and blinded her. Any words she tried to summon up came out as a choked sound.

"Get into the car. Quickly." James told her firmly. He leaned back and watched her approach the car as though it were a bomb about to go off. She opened the door in a rush and climbed in before she could change her mind. He watched her fumble with the seat belt for a long time, injured wrist causing her to falter.

He carefully got a small stack of napkins from his glove compartment and held them out to her, ensuring she could see every telegraphed movement, "Would you allow me to buckle you in? You are hurt." Then a longer hesitation before adding, "Would you like me to take you to the police department?"

As always, his voice just seemed calm and careful. At least until mention of the police department. Then there was a silent disquiet about him. Lyric claimed the napkins and gave up on the belt, just nodding shakily and gesturing to the belt before she favored her wrist.

With all of the effort she could muster, she finally formed a response, "I don't know how much it would help. It didn't help much last time Stephen..." Her voice sounded raw. She leaned her head against the frame of the car window as the cold air blew over her face.

"Your shop was the one that had caught on fire in Maryland, correct? Mysterious circumstances and no proof as to what actually caused the fire. He has now physically assaulted you. It will at least be documented." He spoke evenly as he drove her into the heart of Pius. If he noticed her staring at him, he didn't seem bothered by it.

The unasked question hung heavy in the air, "I keep up on current events. Especially where that... man is concerned." He supplied softly.

Somehow his calm helped her to scrape together her own. The woman wiping at her eyes and nose, "Ah. Yeah, it had been a big thing in the news for a hot second. No evidence as to where the fire started. It wasn't electrical. Not a gas leak. Not even something left behind to show it was the ignitor. Just... fire." She shook and pulled the coat tightly around her.

The memory was one she tried to avoid, but months later and it was still a fresh pain. The feeling of smoke suffocating her and burning her eyes. The feeling of burns over her skin and the smell of burnt hair and flesh. The groaning of wood and brick as supports started to weaken. It had been so fast. Too fast. She still didn't remember how she survived it. By all means, she shouldn't have.

James considered her for a long moment and then looked ahead, "But *you* know who did it." He asked as he waited at a stop light. Red causing Lyric's features to seem far more severe as she relived her moment of horror. Fingers thrummed on the steering wheel. Something was nagging on his conscience. It happened often similar to when he had first met Dr. Melanthios. It was repeated when he had encountered others.

She looked at him, "I know." Then she chewed on her lip, "Is Stephen really Doctor Melanthios' brother?" That got more of a reaction than she had ever seen out of the male. She watched him sneer from anger. Obviously displeased enough that it made her curl away from him reflexively. That reaction was enough to make James takes deep breaths and murmur an apology.

"Unfortunately, yes. He has two, but the other one keeps to himself. Idris still gets into trouble, but he doesn't set stores on fire." He had a feeling his boss didn't even know Stephen was in town yet. Something that needed to be amended quickly. Every time Stephen came around to cause trouble and Tahvo showed off spectacular anger. Something told him that this time around it wouldn't work out as easily. Not when Tahvo was anywhere near what Stephen wanted badly enough to stalk across state lines.

"They don't look or even act the same. I can't believe they are brothers at all." Lyric admitted and she frowned at her hands, "I am afraid of what Stephen will do to T- Doctor Melanthios. I don't want him to get hurt or his animals. Last time I pissed Stephen off I barely survived it." Her hand absently rubbed against her leg. Eyes closing as the phantom pain was intermingling with the new pain of her wrist.

"Stephen doesn't enjoy being told no." James stated as he pulled in front of the station. Another study of her before looking up at the station, "Although most times the Doctor is gentle, he will stand up to his older brother. One thing you do not do is threaten safe haven he has built. Nor those that he has under his care." He let that sink in before continuing, "Last time Stephen came anywhere near here, he left with a broken nose. The idiot had thought it was smart to cut one of the fences open so that some of the dogs could get out." Luckily Tahvo made sure to have every animal chipped as well as special tags to keep track of them all and in case any of them knew how to be Houdini.

Lyric looked up at the station and then wrapped her arms around her. In the dark, the neon sign that announced 'Police' right over it so people knew where it was should have given her comfort, "Mr. Cheroni, would you please come inside with me? I don't want to be alone." And she felt like she would be there all night.

James tore his eyes away from the station to look at the woman beside him. Wrist cradled to her chest. He weighed the pros and cons of walking into the station as he was and sighed. It helped that he worked with a man who helped care for the local K9 unit. Even if their owners left... much to be desired. He withheld a sigh and he nodded, motioning for her to lean away from the window so that he could roll it up.

"Would you be alright if I called Doctor Melanthios and let him know his brother is in town? If he is around to cause trouble, we should make sure the animals are safe." That and if anything happened to Lyric, he was fairly certain that Tahvo would blame himself for any harm that came of her. Especially given he could see how distracted the doctor had become after Lyric's last visit.

"Yeah, it would be a good idea to keep him and the animals safe. Thank you, Mr. Cheroni." Lyric said softly. She was relieved that she wouldn't be going inside alone. About to climb out of the car first, she blinked when James placed his hand on her arm for her to wait before he climbed out and rounded about the car to open the door and offer his hand to her.

"You may call me James, Miss Helios." His voice a little softer as he helped her stand out of the car. Her hand was trembling as it gripped his tightly.

"Thank you, James. You may call me Lyric then. I am not too huge on formalities. I have been trying to make it a habit for Doctor Melanthios' sake. He seems to prefer it." She watched James smile knowingly and she drew her hand away as he walked with her up to the doors.

It took a while and there were a lot of asked questions. Lyric felt cold in the place, even with the cup of coffee sitting in the little Styrofoam cup that probably was probably old and bitter. She was glad to know James would be waiting for her in the lobby when she was all done. Being in a strange place where she knew no one at all was disconcerting, although she was glad they didn't question if Stephen was actually causing her trouble or not. They all seemed to know of the man and promised to keep an eye out on him and do regular drive-by checks past her complex to ensure he wouldn't be stalking about her home or workplace.

They asked her to call them if there was any more attempted contact from him. They even offered to put a restraining
order since he had assaulted her. It made him a potential
threat upon her person. Lyric knew a paper wouldn't really
stop someone determined to hurt her, but she guessed it
was the thought that counted. By the time it was all done,
all Lyric desperately wanted was sleep.

When she came out to the lobby, she froze in place as
she saw James talking to Tahvo quietly. A study of Tavho
and she could see a few scattering similarities, but she was
certain he must have favored one of his parents more than
his brother did. When Tahvo looked over at her, she didn't
see anything of the leering face that had been over her. Not
the person that was angry at her for turning him down. She
saw a concerned one that looked relieved that she was in
one piece. He had been worried for her?

Lyric had wondered if James told him anything about how
she knew Stephen. She stood awkwardly as she tugged the
coat around her shoulders as Tahvo approached her. The
warmth of his hand was almost startling as she realized
just how cold she felt. She was exhausted and his presence
immediately made her feel safe.

"Did he hurt you?" Tahvo asked her with a soft urgency. He
could feel her cold clammy skin and how much she was
trembling. It made him absolutely furious that his brother
could scare her like this. He still didn't know about the fire
Stephen set in her old shop. Just that James suggested he

ask her later about what Stephen had done. It wasn't his story to share after all. Something Tahvo could respect.

Lyric shook her head, "No... well... Not... not too badly. He mostly startled me more than anything. He shoved me and I think just bruised my wrist. I kicked him really hard in the knee, so I know he is limping." She saw a flicker of anger and then relief in Tahvo's eyes. As she shuddered hard at remembering the way Stephen slammed her, a soft aborted sound of fear that threatened to escape. Then she felt his arms wrap tightly around her and hug her to him. Normally she would have run or felt suffocated, but in his arms she felt like she could mold herself against him to hide from nightmares.

Her voice was soft as Lyric asked, "Did you come all the way out here for me?"

"Yes. I have Officer Bowet keeping an eye on the clinic and house for me. She won't let anything happen to the animals." Tahvo was glad she was alright. He was also glad she knew how to get out of a bad situation. The knee was a hell of a place to aim for to keep someone from running after you. "Do you have somewhere safe to stay?"

"Not really. My mother would never ... I live alone. I don't want to be alone again if he...." Lyric trailed off softly.

"Then you are staying at my place." Tahvo told her suddenly before realizing he was choosing for her. He cringed and quickly amended, "Sorry, I mean... if you want to, you can stay with me until this gets sorted out. I would hate for you to be in danger. I will gladly deal with any wrath your mother decides to unleash."

"You really don't mind?" Lyric asked. Given their conversation of earlier... she sniffed and then hugged him tightly, "Thank you, Tahvo." And then she drew away enough to look at James, "And thank you for bringing me here, James. I don't know where I would have gone if you hadn't driven by." She didn't know where to go. Didn't know what was a safe place.

James gave a small nod and a thin smile, "I am glad I was in the right place to have assisted. If you wish, ask Doctor Melanthios for my number. If you are ever in need of help, I will do my best to give it. Please be safe tonight. Both of you." He gave a bow of his head and then left the lobby.

After ensuring that the police had everything needed and his contact information, Tahvo led Lyric outside to his car. It wasn't a car that was sleek and stylish, but instead looked sturdy and safe. A vehicle one could transport animals in if needed. She let him help her into the sports vehicle before he got into it himself. After ensuring she was alright and if she needed anything to eat, Tahvo started for home.

Lyric watched as things passed outside of her window, appetite non-existent, "How much did J- Mr. Cheroni tell you?"

"Just that Stephen had attacked you and that you knew him from before you came here. He had said the rest was for you to share. I won't push if you are uncomfortable." Gods knew Tahvo had his own problems he didn't openly discuss.

There was a small nod at that and she rubbed at her leg with the palm of her hand, "I met him before I moved out here. It has almost been a year I guess... but when I was in Maryland I had..." She trailed off and frowned, "I dated a lot. I always thought dates were the precursor to actually being in a relationship with someone. A way to get to know someone to see if you would want to spend time further or not. He was someone I had turned down and he was insistent. He kept trying to hit on me all of the time. Followed me to classes and my workplace."

"He got angry when I accepted an offer for a date from a girl I knew. She was sweet, but nothing really came of it beyond spending the night at her place. I thought he finally got the clue that I wasn't interested and hadn't heard from him for a few days. Then I had seen him in the old shop and ... I turned around and there was fire." Lyric's voice dropped down to a hushed whisper, "There was an investigation, but I couldn't prove he was there. I had been by myself. There was no evidence as to what caused the fire. The shop was my mother's and she blamed me for it. Blamed me for being 'loose' and inviting trouble. She is making me pay back the money from having to buy a new shop and relocate as well. The old place had become condemned."

Tahvo cursed loudly, causing her to jump at the sudden ve-hement anger he had. That made him cringe and shoulders drop, "I am sorry for yelling. I just... I knew he was trouble and violent with me. I never thought he would ever go to such an extent to stalk someone else. I would apologize about him, but I know very well that his behavior is only his fault." It was something he would never take the blame for. Stephen always tried to guilt him for that and Tahvo would never take it.

Lyric looked at him and smiled faintly, "I would be telling you it wasn't your fault anyway. I am glad neither of you are alike. I would never have guessed you two were related. You are so nice." She watched him seem to be rolling ideas through his head. Had to wonder what had him thinking so hard. Still, he did acknowledge her words with a glance towards her and a thin smile returned.

"I do my best to present myself as a decent human being. Stephen always acted as though he were some sort of god and should be worshipped as such. He thinks everyone should give him whatever he wants. Honestly, I think any god who acts like that would be a very terrible at his job unless of course his aspect is that of a lack of self-control."

Lyric laughed quietly at that. Gods she was so exhausted. She closed her eyes and listened to the car running and the sounds of other cars driving past at night. It seemed like a lively enough city. Given her day of delivering had been busy, she knew the nursery would do well. Especially as one of the older ones was leaving. Such a sweet woman too, "I am sorry you got wrapped up in my crap."

"Don't apologize for him or your mother. They should know better than to try to control the life of someone else like that. Everyone should have the freedom to choose, not get trapped." Tahvo's voice was soft as he said that.

He looked over at her and smiled, "Why don't you try and catch a nap. I will wake you up when we get there." He watched as she nodded quietly and started to fall asleep.

He drove in that quiet for a while. Purposefully taking a bit of the long way to get home. First he passed by the plant nursery to make sure it was still standing. If Stephen was there, he didn't see him. He eventually got them home and guided the car up the drive and into the garage and turned the car off. The silence was nearly deafening.

Tahvo studied the still sleeping woman and then quietly moved around the car and unbuckled her. Surprised that she remained asleep, he scooped her up into his arms and cradled her close to his chest. She was dead to the world as she just merely murmured his name and snuggled against him. A soft chuckle and he carefully moved through the house and up the stairs, tucking her into his bed. The only thing he did remove was her shoes, he didn't want to disturb her sleep. She looked so small and frail in that moment. He knew better, but he still wanted to protect her.

Asteri and Spot poked their heads into the room and Tahvo put his finger up to his lips in a quieting gesture. He approached them and pet them both, "I need you two to keep her company, alright? I am going to check on the clinic and tell Officer Bowet that she can go home now." Spot whined at him and bumped his snout against Tahvo in worry. "I will be alright. I need you to keep her safe for me. Stephen tried hurting her." With that name spoken, Spot growled low and became more alert and trotted beside the bed and hopped up to lay at the foot of it. Asteri followed and jumped up and snuggled against Lyric's side.

Tahvo smiled at the sight and mouthed a silent thanks before going down the stairs and walking out to get to the clinic. He saw Bowet's car and approached it. He noted she wasn't inside and instead went into the clinic. Then he frowned as he looked around the lobby. She wasn't in there either. He slowly walked through, his gait changing into being more prepared for a potential fight. He could hear the dogs now. They were loud and alarmed. That made him rush down the hall and turn down the hall that led to all of the dog kennels. Which looked more like a massive play room divided up into parts. All of them were pawing at their gates and barking loudly. Tahvo saw what they were barking at and he swore. He quickly moved further into the room and knelt down at the woman leaning back against one of the fences. Bowet was conscious, but she had blood oozing down from her forehead and bruising forming along her eye.

"Your brother is itching for a castration isn't he?" Bowet muttered as she waved off Tahvo. She pushed herself up onto her feet. A growl on her lips and she touched her fingers on her lip to check it. No blood from there at least. A look around the room and she sighed, "I am going to end him when I get ahold of him."

"I share that sentiment, Bowet. Unfortunately, you will have to get in line." She had her temper still, which assured Tahvo she would be alright, "Do you think he hurt anyone else?"

"I don't think so. The dogs started snarling at him when he got me. I did manage to shoot him in the shoulder. Not sure if your friend hit him hard enough in the knee. He looked like he was running just fine." She sighed and straightened, "But he will get into deep shit for assault. I suggest closing up tomorrow until we can give you a heads up on what is going on. Make sure the animals are all oka-"

Tahvo looked puzzled by her sudden stop in talking as they watched a small cockatiel scuttle past the open door down the hall. The vet groaned and sighed, "Can you help me make sure none of the other animals got out please? I have to go catch Muse. I think Stephen was trying to leave all of the cages open again. With my luck the alligator will see the cockatiel and think he is lunch."

Bowet snorted at the mental image and nodded, "I have back up coming as well so if there is any animal wrangling we need to do, they will be here to help." She watched him leave before she looked at the dogs and gave a soft hushing sound. They seemed to settle before she went about the property. The other Officer Bowet showed up as well as a couple of others and they helped Tahvo calm all of the loose animals and rounded them up.

The most concerning part in it all was the horses. Stephen had let them out as well and despite getting most accounted for, one was still missing. Tahvo helped calm them, but he looked at the empty stall that once had one of the newer guests. Something told him that something was wrong and the others must have felt it as well. They were going to have to find the chip number and keep an eye out for the horse named Black Pearl. That shouldn't have been *too difficult* to locate.

After ensuring everything was alright, both Officer Bowets promised him they would find the horse. The larger of the pair was Cecilia's husband. The male was dark brown and had all of hair in tight braids that were all drawn back to the back of his head with a few braids looped around the mass to secure it. His expression was severe and he had been on edge ever since he saw the injuries his wife had. Tahvo was pretty sure if Cecilia didn't get ahold of Stephen first, Orion would.

Tahvo finally assured himself everything would be alright and set the alarms before walking home. It was cold out this late, but at the moment he didn't mind. He was angry enough to not care. He slipped back inside and checked in on the puppies and cat in their room before quietly making his way to his own room. Spot lifted his head up as soon as he stepped in. His hand gently ruffled his short fur and scratched behind the ear. Asteri slept soundly beside Lyric. At least no one was hurt here. He went to the attached bathroom after grabbing clothes to sleep in and ambled off. He was never going to get any sleep with feeling as tense as he was.

He tried to think of a way to deal with the situation at hand while hot water poured over him. He was in there until the water started running cold. Which meant he had been in there way too long. Exhausted and worried, Tahvo dried off and pulled on warm pajama pants and made his way back to the bed. Given the giant size of it, he had space to slip into it and look over the large space at Lyric beside him. He set his alarm so that he could wake up early enough to make sure she could get to work on time without a fuss. It didn't leave much sleep for him, but he promised himself that he would keep her safe. The loss of sleep was well worth it.

The dreams weren't peaceful this time. They still felt like odd memories, but this time it was clearer. He was seeing it from the view of the one he guessed was named Hades. The one across from him was glaring at him with cold blue eyes. Hair was golden and bright. The man could have almost have been handsome if there wasn't anger marring the perception of Hades as he glared at the other male.

"You have so many others you could go be lecherous scum with. Why didn't you just leave her alone, Zeus? You made her think it was me! Have you any idea what you've done?"

"Oh relax, it isn't like you don't have half the year to play with her all you want. Frankly with all that time. I'm surprised you two don't have children yourselves. Tell me, Brother, who would the kids stay with when she isn't here?"

"This is not some kind of game! You are a god, but you have absolutely no respect for the title or the people you are supposed to be ruling over. The only reason they are not laughing at your face is because they fear you. Know that I do not fear you. You are going to regret your actions."

"What are you going to do to me, Hades? Kill me?"

"Perhaps in a manner of speaking, I will. The world is changing, Zeus. People start getting bored and start looking for something else to worship. It happens all of the time and you know it. Soon we will be mere whispers and myths instead of historical fact." Hades marched forward, the swaths of fabric draped around him billowed and flowed like the rivers that cut through the realm that shared his name, "I will just be there to usher it along, and when the world forgets who we are, then your power will be no more."

Zeus barked laughter at him, "There are great temples to my person. Stories written about my conquests. Statues of my great visage. Songs and tales about all I have done.

Children that I have begotten! How would you seek to erase me from history?"

"Stone crumbles, Brother mine. Scrolls burn. Songs and tales forgotten and misplaced. People die and bloodlines end." Hades said coldly. His anger settling into calculation. It was all the warning he would ever give his brother. This act had been the last straw, "I do not fear taking you down with me. I will erase us all to ensure that we are free of all of your petty conquests and the consequences that have come of it."

The humor vanished from Zeus' face as he glared, "You would not dare. You would lose your precious Persephone. Your precious field and hound. You labor too much over these pathetic souls to abandon them so easily."

"I am resourceful. Count your days, Brother. Our time is coming to an end."

If there was anything more to the dream, Tahvo didn't get to see it. He sat up straight and stared into the dark room as his phone bleated a goat sound loudly into the room. He pawed at his end table until it turned off before looking over beside him. Even in the dark, he could see the warmth of the eyes staring at him as she cuddled against his side. He wasn't sure who had moved to the other or if it was mutual, but he realized her leather clad arm was draped across his waist.

"Sorry, if my alarm startled you." He told her in a soft whisper, "Did you sleep well?" He idly moved his hand to smooth over her hair. It was nice to wake up to such bright warm eyes after an oddly vivid dream like that. Dreams seemed to happen on the rare occasions that Stephen showed up. Franky, this Zeus reminded him a lot of his brother.

"I did. Thank you." She snuggled against him a bit more until she realized what she was doing. Lyric stared at the shadows of the room before speaking again, "Am I allowed to ask you to pretend I never said we shouldn't try to date anymore? I feel like a jerk for it."

Tahvo blinked and then smiled down at her tentatively, "It would make the current situation and my feelings a little less awkward if I was speaking on behalf of my own emotions. I would prefer it if you were comfortable and sure about things before making any decisions." He leaned back in the bed and reached over to flick on a dim light that gave the room a warm glow without blinding them.

His room was warm in tone. Walls were painted a deep garnet with cream curtains to soften the darkness of the room. Copper paint colored the moldings and was the primary color of his current bed set. The bed frame itself looked like it was branches made of wrought iron painted bronze. Copper, bronze, and gold leaves were cut and placed in an artful way that made it almost seem alive. It cast interesting shadows on the walls.

"You have had an eventful couple of days. I would not wish for you to make any choices you would regret. I am willing to wait until you are ready." Although part of him really did hope she would eventually want to date. Which was probably foolish to hope for. He had to wonder if he should even be laying there with her like he was; Hand playing with her hair with such familiarity.

His words were considered and Lyric closed her eyes at the feeling of his fingers in her hair. She wondered time it was, but part of her did not want to care. Reluctantly, she fished her phone from her pocket and frowned at the time and then the low battery, "I guess I should get up and start getting ready. Are you okay if I use your shower?"

"I am fine with it. I also have some extra toothbrushes in the bathroom. I always buy ahead." He admits with a smile. Of course, all of his things smelled like peppermint, but he hoped it would not bother her. He shifted to sit up again slowly after she started to get up, "I will show you where everything is and then I can drive you to work. I promise not to do anything to aggravate your mother too much beyond existing as I do."

Lyric noted his wry smile and pulled off the jacket, "I still need to get different clothes. Can you take me to my place? I can always get a shower there instead." Mind you compared to his house her apartment was embarrassingly small.

He nodded and moved to get up, stifling a yawn. He really wanted a lot more sleep. His main goal though was to make sure Lyric got to work safely. The rest could honestly wait. Tahvo stretched and started to get his clothes out of the closet. There was a considering look at his clothes as he thought about something, "Lyric, how close were you to finishing paying off your loan to your mother?"

"Before the fire? I had about three years yet. I had a lot of high paying contracted jobs. I was helping do research and was substituting at a school for their science department. I was paying a little over a thousand per month. That is without interest thankfully. I was aiming for ten-twelve years and then be done with it. I was living with her then. After, I couldn't stand it anymore and got the apartment, but until I can get myself established here, I am set back quite a bit. I owe her for the cost of the new shop too. Insurance only covers so much." Her shoulders sagged, "I had to quit my other jobs and move, it wasn't safe where I was. Looks like Stephen found me anyway."

There was a long consideration and he looked over at her, "I could always use another assistant. With your knowledge on biology, it would benefit the clinic and shelter."

Was he offering her a job? Lyric shook her head as she pulled her shoes on, "It would break the agreement with my mother. I am not allowed to work anywhere but the shop else I lose everything. Not after the fire." Not like she was particularly attached to anything, but she did enjoy a roof over her head and even food on the table.

Tahvo didn't look at her as he spoke again, "Well, I have heard of a thing called possession being nine-tenths of the law. Not to mention I have a relatively large house and plenty of rooms. There is a lot of dog hair all over the place of course and I tend to keep some odd hours, but it would technically be *my* place. So she can't take that from you. It would work out for you until you have your debts settled. Then you could move anywhere you would like and work wherever you like." He tried to keep his tone casual as he spoke. He knew how expensive student loans could be. He was lucky enough to have been able to pay his off. Lucky enough to be able to have a place as successful as this. He knew he needed help, but he was very selective about who he trusted with the lives he cared for.

Lyric just stared at him, not even looking away as he changed. Her jaw would have been on the floor right then. It took her a moment for her to pick it up. She wished it would have only been because he was changing. He *did* look nice.

"You are absolutely serious, aren't you? Why? Why would you help me? It isn't because of Stephen is it?"

There was a loud snort that sounded anything but gentlemanly and Tahvo looked over at her. If he was more awake the fact she was watching him change would have kicked in, "Gods no, I would not sully this with his idiocy. Everyone needs a choice, Lyric. I admit, your choices are heavily due to financial reasons, but you wouldn't be restricted here. I certainly would never dream of telling you where you can go, how to dress, or if you should date or not nor who."

"Wait, date? What, like if I was living here and we decided not to... you know... date each other. You would be okay with me dating someone else?" Lyric frowned at him then. Now she watched him closely as his shoulders sagged.

"Okay with it in the sense that I will respect your choices. I may be disappointed that it is not me, but you have the right to say no. I am being kind to be kind, not just to win your good graces and hope one day to get into your pants." Tahvo explained as he ran a brush through his hair and tied it back. He canted his head at her and added, "I believe the difference between a 'nice guy' and a nice person is the intent behind ones actions."

"If you ask the Bowets, they were guests here for a short while once when they lost their home due to a very nasty snowstorm that collapsed their roof due to snowfall." He hoped that would assure her to some degree.

"I believe you." Lyric finally said. He really was so careful about everything, Tahvo hadn't given her any reason to doubt him. It still felt so cruel to take advantage of his kindness and also push his heart away. She frowned and studied him, "Can I think about it for a few days? I mean... I might need to stay here for the next few days anyway when I am not at work. I don't want another run-in with the pyro stalker."

The fact she believed him was a relief. People were so very right to be suspicious of such altruism. Too many used it as a trap, "You may stay here as long as you need. You may think of it as a test run if you'd like."

Ah, and he hadn't even gotten to mentioning what happened at the clinic yet. It was probably best not to worry her before work. She had enough on her plate without blaming herself for Stephen coming after his place of work too. "I will be closing the clinic to the public today anyway and doing routine checks of all the animals. So if you need anything at all today, please call me."

"I will, I promise. Let's get to my place first. If I pack a bag, could you bring it back here for me? Then I can come here right after work and have all of my things that I will need." She smiled softly at him. She really did not want to even chance Stephen waiting for her. Lyric was honestly touched by his generosity. It was help that she really needed that she never dared to find help for. It was causing a wear and tear on her mental state as it was. Little rebellions cost her and sometimes made her question if any of it was truly worth it.

Tahvo readily agreed to taking care of that errand for her. Then he proceeded to show her where the food was to feed the dogs and cat before they left. Between the two of them, they got the animals fed before they made their way to her apartment.

When they got to the building, Tahvo remained close and on the look-out for anything unusual as she led him into her place and took him up to what he would have considered an efficiency apartment. Her bedroom was a living room all in one. Just enough space for a futon and a coffee table that doubled as a nightstand. A small monitor and disk player for her movies. The kitchen was tiny as well and didn't even have a table in it. The only other room was the bathroom which she quickly bee-lined for and vanished in.

He looked around the small place and felt like an awkward giant. He was tall enough to have to duck from the ceiling fan. As it was, it made him nervous enough to try and steer clear of it entirely. Almost as quickly as she vanished into the shower, she was skipping out of it with wet hair hanging around her face in little ringlets plastered to her head and face and only a towel. He stepped back in the small space with his back pressed against a wall to give her space as she rushed around the room. She yanked out a box from under her futon and tossed a t-shirt and jeans as well as underwear and a bra onto it before rushing around and digging around in a tiny closet and throwing a duffel bag behind her and rushing back into the bathroom.

It was like she had entirely forgotten he was there. It made him smile as she rushed around like a frantic cat chasing a red dot. She ran out of her bathroom with an armful of things and dropped them into the duffle. This time she had her towel wrapped around her head and nothing on at all. Which showed off a sprawling gnarled mark along her hip that made him frown. It looked very newly healed. Though he didn't comment on it. Instead Tahvo looked intently at his phone to let her get dressed first. When she was done, he stepped away from the wall.

"How about you let me try to pack some things for you before you trip and hurt yourself." He mused. The owl-like look coming from her when she remembered he was there brought such a heat to her face that he found it utterly charming.

"Ah, actually, can you help pack lunch for me? I have some left overs in my fridge. My lunch box should be on top of the fridge." It would be one less thing for her to fret over. She gave a smile to him as he nodded and walked over to her bitty kitchenette, "Thank you, Tahvo. I will probably be saying that a lot, so I hope you don't get tired of it."

Tahvo frankly couldn't imagine getting tired of hearing her voice, but he kept the comment to himself. Instead he just smiled, getting the lunch box down and looking in her fridge to see that it was sparse. Still, there was a small container of some sort of take out. He shook his head with a chuckle and picked that out and a bottle of water and put it in the bag. A search for utensils gave him several boxes of plastic ones. Unsure of which ones to give her, he just opted for one of each and looked around. Would that even be enough food for her? He was definitely making sure she ate a good dinner tonight.

"Packed!" Lyric announced, unwinding the towel from her hair as she marched back to hang it up on the hook on her bathroom door. The very edges of her hairline had blue and green on it, meaning she managed to refresh her color in that time in the shower. A rushed job given he could see the splotch of color on her neck.

"Same." Tahvo said as he walked to her door, "So, you have everything you need?"

"I think so." She said thoughtfully before she grabbed a couple of worn out books and a couple of movies and shoved them into her bag for extra measure, "There, I should be good now. The rest of it I don't really care about much." She adjusted the one little piece she did actually care about. It shimmered in gold over the collar of her black shirt. It made Tahvo pause as he looked at the necklace.

"Not to be distracted, but what is that?" He didn't know why it caught his attention so. Lyric looked at him quizzically before she glanced down at her own neck. Calloused fingers picked at it as she showed it to him. It looked like a small pomegranate cut open with one half with six cut garnets that looked like arils. The other section had a woman relaxing in the little nook. The gold carved to show the woman nude but relaxed. It was a pure peace looked happy and at ease. The way the tiny details were carved looked like it was meant to actually be someone. Down to the last little carved strand of hair that flowed with the small woman.

"This? I found it on one of my trips abroad. I had gone diving with a few people while in Greece and I found it in the ocean. I mean, I think someone probably lost it somewhere, but I liked it too much and kept it. It is one of my good memories, as I didn't have my mother breathing down my neck."

"That's a pomegranate." Tahvo whispered. He approached with that soft curiosity and his thumb absently brushed against the edge of it with a sort of reverence. The small golden woman looked like the woman Persephone from his dreams. So strange. He shook his head suddenly and smiled at her, "It is a very pretty piece. Perhaps it was meant to be yours."He checked the time then, "We should go, I don't want you to be late again."

"Right." His reaction to it had been very curious. The pendant was soon forgotten as Lyric looked behind her and into the apartment one more time before leaving and locking the door behind them. They made it to his car and he started the vehicle up while she tucked her bag into the back seat. A shudder as the cold air hit her head and she quickly climbed in, pulling his jacket around her. Why couldn't it have come with a hood?

"Brr, I should have dried my hair." Lyric mumbled as he set her lunch box in her lap. Then blinked as he tucked a little money into the side pocket of the zipped bag, "What are you doing?"

"I've seen what you had to eat, Lyric. That is hardly enough food when you work that hard. It's a miracle you haven't blown away in a stiff wind." Tahvo smiled at her good naturedly, "So, if you are still hungry after that, make sure you buy yourself something to eat for lunch. Please? I promise to make dinner when you get home. Can't have my house guest starving now can I?"

"I... well. I guess not. Thank you. You know, if I accept your offer, you are going to have one of the hardest working assistants ever." Lyric smiled at him. She would have to be, with all of his kindness. She certainly would hate to take advantage of Tahvo. "Well, aside from James anyway. I think he might outwork me."

Tahvo laughed as he drove her down to her nursery, "Funny, his boyfriend keeps telling me how lazy he is." It was all in good jest. No one could rightfully accuse the man of being lazy by any means. James put in more hours than anyone rightfully should. He never complained or argued unless it was Tahvo trying to send him home early. Perhaps having another assistant would give James a break and assure the male that Tahvo wouldn't work himself to death.

Lyric laughed and then sighed as she saw the shop come up. She was a little early. Which meant she could prepare for helping the school and taking in orders. Work would be a good distraction at least. Though her skin still crawled at the thought of being alone where Stephen could find her.

"Thank you again, Tahvo. Seriously. I would be a sleepless mess today if you and James hadn't come and helped. Thank James for me too please?" She hesitated and leaned over to kiss his cheek, "I look forward to dinner tonight. Don't work too hard!" She then moved to escape out of the passenger seat and started approaching the nursery. Tahvo rolled down his window to shout out after her.

"Make sure to call me when you are done! I'll come pick you up!" He smiled as she shouted a promise to call him and she skipped along inside. Tahvo smiled at her and shook his head as he drove off back home. As soon as he pulled into his garage, he blinked as his phone sounded off from a text message.

'Hey Tahvo, it is Lyric. I figured since I work by myself, you might get worried. So I am going to try and message you in-between deliveries! Not while driving, I promise!'

A blink and he laughed when he got another message.

'By the way... can we have cheeseburgers for dinner? I haven't had those in a while. Like real ones. Not the scrawny cheap things from the fast food restaurant. I don't even think those things are real beef.'

He grinned and messaged her back a yes and then added for her to be careful. Tahvo could feel exhaustion pulling at him. Despite being so tired, he checked over the clinic first. Ensuring that everyone inside was alright and proceeded to check the barn as well. No signs nor news of the missing horse yet.

Finally, he made his way back home. Exhaustion dragged on him. Just a little sleep and then he was going to go to the store and get some food. Tahvo just hoped that it would be a quiet day. So long as Stephen stayed far away from people for a few days, he could figure out how to deal with the idiot. Maybe he would get lucky and someone would track him down and knock his ass flat. Maybe Pearl trampled the waste of carbon.

Another feeding for the puppies before he set an alarm and merely kicked off his shoes and flopped into the bed. Sleep claimed him quickly after texting Lyric and for a few hours, he was dead to the world.

5

The Underworld long ago...

Hades looked beside him as Persephone laid against him. Her head rested against his thigh as she cuddled a small sleeping bundle against her. While he was glad to see her happy and content, he couldn't help but feel a pang of anger knowing where the baby, Zagreus, came from. Persephone had known too as soon as he found out and told her that it hadn't been him. He remembered the fear she had when he told her.

Persephone had waited for him to cast her away and never allow her back. Despite his anger at his brother, he was never angry at her. How could he be? Zeus did such things to so many people, and his wife was but another victim. Never did he wish for her to feel same over the god violating her trust for his own pleasure.

Instead he calmed down enough to reassure her that he was not angry at her. So long as she was safe and happy, he would be as well. The occasional glimmers of guilt for what she could not control broke his heart into pieces. The fact that she had been used and been made afraid. Made to distrust her own mind and hesitance every time she wanted to reach for him. As though he weren't really himself. She wanted a child, but not with anyone but Hades. Now she held the byproduct of trickery, yet she only gave love. After all, it wasn't the child's fault. Which made the subject Hades was about to bring up very difficult.

"Persephone," He said softly. Fingers trailed through her rich brown hair. In the sunlight he remembered the highlights of red in the curls. Something he could never see down here, "Had you another chance to do things differently, would you have chosen to get to know me on your own terms instead of by force?"

Persephone looked up at him with blue eyes as soft as the morning sky. His question was considered before she frowned, "You were terrifying to me at first. I rarely ever saw you outside of the Underworld. I don't know if I would have ever had the opportunity. My mother always kept me close enough to suffocate me."

Hades frowned and his voice became even softer, "Are you ever angry at me for sweeping you away as I had? That you didn't have a choice in our meeting each other?"

Now she knew something was wrong. The goddess sat up and frowned at him, arms adjusting the sleeping baby as she looked at her husband, "My love, why are you asking me these things? What troubles you?"

How was he supposed to tell her that he planned on wiping out their whole pantheon? That the anger at his brother was the last straw? He averted his gaze, but Hades knew he could never lie to her. Hiding information was the last thing he could do to her, not when she deserved so much better, "What if you could choose to come and go as you wished? Where we wouldn't have to spend half a year apart?" His expression looked lost as he looked to her, "What if you could have chosen to be with me without being kidnapped? I was not fair to you..." Hades felt he was barely any better than his brother.

"Oh, Hades." Her voice soft as she cupped his face with her fingers. Persephone wanted to make him feel better somehow. Except as soon as she looked into his eyes, she knew he was hurting to a depth she could not reach, "You know how much I hate to leave and if you are worried you are like your brother, you are not." She looked up into his eyes. He looked like he was guilty of some atrocious act.

Fingers curled against her hand and he admired the love she held. Persephone was such a brave soul. This was the woman who chose to eat the food of the Underworld. Chose him but... some days he wondered if she had really wanted to or if she felt she had no choice but to succumb to his wishes. That he was the lesser evil between being trapped with her mother or trapped with him.

"I had... considered the possibility of wiping our pantheon out of the memories of mortals." He finally told her. Hades watched the information sink in and fear fill her eyes.

"That would kill us!" She shrieked and actually tumbled back on the bed a rush to get away from him. The baby boy in her arms cried loudly from the shock. Seeing her run from him crushed him.

"Please listen. I had thought it out in its entirety. I plan for reincarnation. For all of us. How much has the world suffered for Zeus thinking only with his loins?" Despite his need to hold her, the god did not chase her. Instead his hands rested in his lap where the sheets pooled at his waist.

"We could have the freedom to choose. To see each other whenever we wished." If they found each other at all, "Or you could find someone far better for you. Someone who could give you children and you could be married to them instead of the King of the Dismal Land of the Dead."

"Are you are so worried about six months out of the year!? If you did this, there is a chance I would never see you ever again!" Her voice cracked from panic as she stared at him. Arms hugged the screaming baby close to her chest. In that moment she did not see her husband nor the baby she loved. The baby that Hades still helped care for without an ounce of hatred, "I don't want anyone else but you! I don't even want to-" She broke her words off and just finally stared at him in utter horror.

Her husband looked so dejected sitting there. Then her shoulders sagged, "You are always so alone when I am gone." Her voice soft. Persephone was stating a fact rather than a question, but still she saw him nod, "Whereas I am with others when I leave here." She was never really alone. Him on the other hand... he was presented as cold and angry. Yes he had all of that, but she knew he was lonely. He had about as much free choice in the matter as she did. Sure, they could choose to go against the better wishes of others, but things would go so horribly wrong. So how was this idea any better? "What happens with all of the souls already here and their families still waiting to join them?"

"There are other pantheons in which their afterlife is termed Underworld. Hel's is not dissimilar to mine. Those with good souls go to a place to live out the remainder of their afterlife in peace. Those who are cruel would be punished. I think Charon would be out of the job sadly as they lack a river. Perhaps he would retire and do something for himself." He explained to her, "And in time, some of those souls may have a chance to reincarnate. Find love again, family again, peace again. The world will grow bigger."

How much of his words was to reassure himself that it would work? An eternity with half of his time being utterly alone that was not of his choice. He could have honestly gone to war with her mother over it all. Yet, he had not. There was a pained look to her son. Choices would have to be made. If she told him it would be alright...

"Why are you telling me? The very thought of losing any of this terrifies me." Eyes were glassy. Panic and fear settled to become a deep sadness. Persephone couldn't understand why he would even consider acting upon the idea. Much less tell her the terrible things he would think of doing.

Hades looked to her with glassy eyes after looking up from his empty hands, "I want you to be able to choose what I do next. What you want from me. This means your freedom as much as mine or anyone else's. Even the Fates will not be able to control what we do. I want you to have the freedom to decide on where your path takes you. A chance for sunlight and warmth in all of your days. I refuse to be selfish and dare to decide on your behalf" He shuddered from emotion, but never moved towards her. Hades did not want to force her decision.

Persephone breathed slowly, "A choice for me because... you want my freedom. You are willing to end an entire pantheon for me? Even if my path does not end with you?" Her voice soft as she shifted to shuffle on her knees back towards him. Careful not to touch him just yet. When he nodded she considered him, "But you mentioned all gods. So we would all have a chance for reincarnation? Even the souls here would have such a chance?" He nodded again. Persephone was not so much impressed that he thought it all through. More that he thought of everyone involved. Her eyes went down to the baby, "What about..."

"Reincarnation, although I cannot... guarantee that he will be your child again. I am sorry, my light." Hades told her gently. When she took one of his hands, he stilled. The god didn't want to startle his goddess. He felt her draw his hand up to rest over her heart where the gold necklace hung between her breasts. The gleaming cut garnets and the carved detail of her person on it shone brightly before his hand covered it.

"Perhaps whatever gods reign in the future will smile kindly upon us and make Zagreus yours when I find you again." Persephone told him softly. A shift of weight as she rose up and kissed him softly on his lips. A few tears slid down her cheeks. Still terrified, but she also understood what he meant to do. The world was changing, their stories were becoming scrambled. So many accounts now that the truth of what did and did not happen were obscured or already lost. Their names used less and less. It was only a matter of time.

That kiss was so soft and delicate, his heart hurt at the very thought of not being able to find her again. To not have his kindred spirit at his side to delight him with her laughter and songs and her utter wrath, "Does that mean you are agreeing to this plan?"

Persephone looked at her son who sniffled from the upset. Pain lanced her heart and she already mourned, "I will not agree to this without thinking upon it, but tell me your plan anyway. Tell me how I am to help."

6

Earth, Present.

Tahvo awoke with a yawn when his alarm went off. He blinked blearily as he reached over and realized he wasn't touching his phone on the end table, but his floor. If there had been any dreams, he didn't recall them. There was a slow blink at Spot licking at his face. "I must have slept badly." He muttered. Hand ruffled the ears of Spot before sitting up.

His whole body ached as he sat up. A groan as he realized how much he hurt from falling out of the bed. A search for his phone and he finally grabbed it, checking the messages. Just as promised, Lyric messaged him between deliveries. A smile coming to his features as every one of them hoped he slept well. No, he so wasn't telling her that gravity wrestled him to the floor.

'I am awake now. Did you want to bring your car here after work?'

'Gods no. I hate this tiny car. Mom can keep the stupid thing. I can't even begin to imagine what if you drove this.'

'I might have more back problems.'

'I think you'd have less than if you weren't falling off the bed all of the time.'

That made Tahvo blink slowly and he looked up to see Lyric wearing an amused smile at his doorway. Confusion in his eyes as he looked at his phone again and stared as he realized what time it actually was. It wasn't seven in the morning. It was *seven at night*.

"I slept the entire day?"

"Pretty hard too." Lyric responded.

"I know I was tired but..." He never slept like that. Not unless he was seriously sick. There was a frown and he pushed himself up to his feet. The world turned sideways and he started tilting away from the bed. Lyric was suddenly there supporting his weight. With great care she moved to set him down on the edge of the bed. Tahvo shuddered and closed his eyes as he tried to settle his stomach that clenched tight.

"You're burning up." Lyric frowned as she felt his forehead. She carefully laid him into the bed and pressed her cool fingers against his cheek. A frown as she looked him over, "Have you eaten at all today?"

Brows knit together as Tahvo thought hard about that, "I... I don't think I've eaten since we had dinner together." He had been distracted. It was a bad habit that he tried to set alarms for to remember to eat. Else he got too focused on everything else going on around him. Hydrating properly was another habit he was bad at. The animals always were tended to first. After that he just forgot to care for himself.

The animals, "Oh, the puppies. I need to feed them." He tried to sit up and blinked as Lyric pushed him back down and tapped the end of his nose.

"I already did that when I got home. I got worried when you didn't respond when you said you would be waking up. So I stopped by for lunch. I went to feed them and that cat that saved them was already nursing them. I guess she took over mom duties. Though might want to supplement later." Lyric moved to help tug his shoes off of him and his socks to help him cool down, "But, later. Last time I saw you, you were still in the bed. I think you were trying to kill your goat alarm in your sleep. I did meet up with James to help him check over all of the animals. I got to meet Cecilia and Orion. They seem really nice."

As she gave him a rundown, he blinked blearily at her. He felt terrible to be honest. He let her help with his shoes as he fumbled with his shirt buttons, "Sorry for the trouble. I didn't make you miss work, did I?"

"Nope, I didn't have much today. Mostly just landscaping for the one school. So I was able to do stuff around here." She smiled at him and sat on the edge of the bed, "Tell you what, I'll go heat up the leftovers, but tomorrow you owe me some burgers?"

He nodded numbly and as she started to stand, Tahvo grasped onto her hand. Exhaustion still tugged at the corners of his mind, "Wake me up when it is done..." He murmured and then added much more softly, "Thank you, my Persephone." Then he passed out again, feet free and shirt spilled open to help him cool down.

That caused Lyric to stare at him and then their hands in between them. How did he know about that name? Lyric never told anyone about her dreams. Maybe she talked in her sleep? Never thought to ask about that. She wished she could only be as lucky as Persephone had been. Hades in her dreams seemed scary, but he had loved her very much, "I wish you could be the Hades to my Persephone. With far less Zeus." She smoothed his black hair with her hand before kissing his forehead and leaving him quickly to heat up the food.

This time there were no chaotic and messy accidents, allowing Lyric to bring the food up on a tray with a water bottle she found. She carefully set it on the end table and moved to shake Tahvo awake.

"Hey, sleeping beauty. I brought you dinner." She watched him struggle to wake up. Carefully, he sat up with Lyric's assistance. Then, she handed him the bottle of water with the cap flipped up and watched him chug it, "Careful. Can't be making yourself sick." When he finished half of it, she smiled at him again.

"Got Tylenol?"

Tahvo nodded and pointed for his bathroom. Leaning against his headboard he watched her vanish off to his bathroom. Some rummaging and then she returned with the pill bottle and popped it open and held out two to him. He took it gratefully and downed more water before leaning his head back. He was a properly functioning adult. Really.

"Thank you, Lyric." He finally managed and looked at the food and smiled at the cut up chicken, "You are eating too, right?"

"Yep, I just have to go and get my plate. I made sure the dogs all had food. Everyone is fed and James said he would be bringing over some groceries so that you don't need to worry about it tomorrow. I didn't know you haven't taken a day off before." She watched him blink owlishly at her. That was the look of someone who didn't understand why he *needed* a day off.

He decided against a fork and stole a piece of the chicken from his plate with his fingers and popped it into his mouth. Tahvo closed his eyes and sighed. Food was good. Edible food was better. Finally, he looked at Lyric who continued to give him a look, "What? I don't have any real reason to go on vacation and emergencies come up all of the time."

"You have alarms on your phone to remember to eat. You work way too hard. Tomorrow, you should take the day off and *relax*. I am sure James, myself, and the others will make sure all of the animals are fed and there if there really is an emergency, *then* you come down. Maybe considering hiring another doctor to help." Lyric watched him pout for a bit and she couldn't help but kiss his cheek, "I'll be right back."

Tahvo nodded and slowly picked at his food. He was starting to feel better before he heard a very loud pounding at the front door. A frown as the thumping continued. Making the dogs start to bark loudly downstairs. Then it got quiet for a long moment before the distinct sound of glass being shattered and he heard Lyric scream.

Despite his head spinning, he launched himself off the bed and stumbled down the hall to the stairs as he saw billowing black smoke flowing up. As he made his way down, he saw source of it in the living room. The dogs barked frantically as he rushed down the stairs and saw Lyric struggling to fight off Stephen. She was hitting as hard as she could, even at the knees and he seemed not to notice what she was doing to him. It was like he was impervious to any and all injury. The look in his brother's eyes were full of what he could only call insanity.

Tahvo saw red and he felt his body thrumming before he bellowed. He charged at his brother and reached for his throat. The sudden grapple was enough to get the brunette to look up at him long enough for Tahvo's fist to connect with his nose. The surprised sibling dropped like a bag of sand. Lyric scrambled away and started to try and yank down the burning drapes to suffocate the flames. Any concern about being hurt didn't seem to register.

Tahvo had no time to act on his worry for her when a force slammed into his jaw and send him staggering. A glare twisted his features when he caught Stephen trying to head for Lyric. Tahvo reached after him and yanked him back hard by the collar of his shirt and tried to use the momentum to send him towards one of the walls.

"Keep your hands off of her, asshole!" Tahvo snarled his words and yanked harder as Stephen tried to fight him. Those large hands coming to try and peel fingers away from cloth or trying to rip the shirt itself to free himself.

"Or what?" Stephen sneered. He tried to instead push forward, but Tahvo was used to dealing with larger animals with a lot more bulk, "Are you going to kill me and everyone else all over again?"

Confusion nearly caused him to lose grip, but Tahvo regained himself and pivoted as he hauled his brother back from the woman. This time he pinned him against the wall, "What the hell are you talking about? I haven't killed anyone! If I did, you sure as hell wouldn't be standing here!"

"Yet here I am! I guess you never thought far enough ahead about what happens if I regained all of my memories did you?" Stephen struggled and tried to push his brother back. Instead the air went out of his lungs when Tahvo punched his gut. The man had not expected his mild-mannered sibling to be this strong.

Memories? Stephen must have finally snapped. Tahvo growled a warning at his brother not to do anything else stupid as he craned his head back to see Lyric stomping out the flames with the blanket they used the other night. Her hair was warped on the ends from the flames. Tahvo then noted her skin was smudged black and grey from the smoke, but she was alive. From where he stood, he saw that she had blood seeping out of a split on her bottom lip as well as some that matted her bright burnt hair.

Seeing her hurt made him return his glare onto his brother, "You are insane, Stephen. Obviously, you have problems that you can't fix yourself. You need help."

"I know *exactly* how to fix it." Stephen snarled. He shoved his brother away with a strength that surprised him. One of Stephen's hands were held up for them to see. Blood coated the back of his hand, but there was no wound on his skin. The sight made Tahvo instinctively touch his face where he was struck and he felt the where it was damp. Lyric was bleeding too and that combination made him feel ill.

"Time to wake up, *Hades.*" Stephen pulled a very small ornate black box out of his jacket and smeared the blood-ied hand over its surface. It looked so familiar. to Tahvo. Suddenly it started to float on its own as though held up by an invisible string. The crimson ichor started to flow and fill the crevices.

A resounding click echoed in the room as though the box was much larger. Lyric exchanged a confused look with Tahvo. That box was something she had only ever seen in a dream. That confusion only lasted for a brief moment as suddenly she was blinded by pain that felt like a splitting migraine between her eyes.

Unfamiliar images drowned out her surroundings her. It was another world that she saw. Centuries of another life slammed into her mind and suffocated her as the pain overtook every bit of her body. It felt like her lungs and heart were being crushed under the sudden weight of it all like a sudden tsunami. The memories and emotions with them assaulted her with a burning fury as Lyric's body trembled on the floor. Her eyes were unfocused and stared across the room where Tahvo was a crumpled heap upon the floor. Stephen stood over him menacingly and fear filled her, shoving that onslaught to the background. Terror for the male unconscious sank claws into her heart.

"Zeus, no!" Lyric then whimpered and the effort and took a shuddering breath. Her body felt like it was brittle glass and the next sudden movement would turn her into sand on the floor.

Please, fates, don't let him die.

As soon as she spoke, Stephen's eyes narrowed on her. He began to stalk forward and she finally realized who he was. What name had spilled from her lips. Fear and underlying anger flooded her, it was almost too much.

"Zeus!"

The realization rocked her. Memories of him violating her trust in her own judgement and ability to determined what was truth or not were swimming in her head. What he had stolen from her. Anger roared through her as he knelt down beside her body as he reached for her. Nausea twisted her stomach as she didn't want him to dare lay a hand on her ever again.

"The one and only, little Seph." He drawled, grabbing her hair roughly and drawing her head up by it, "Did it please you to help destroy your mother? To be the final death of *our* son? Have you slept well these past millennia, you wretched bitch?"

Lyric mustered up the strength to spit at him, "It pleased me to earn a body that was not sullied by *you*. I gave my husband the ability to feel the sunlight every day. *My* son is no longer tainted by your blood. All of your mistakes no longer bear weight on any of us. Your actions no longer mean anything. Zeus, *you* no longer mean anything."

"Well, *your* mistakes, Late Queen of the Underworld, will be the end of you both." He went to lift her head up higher before a blur black and white blur latched itself to his arm with a vicious snarl. Asteri had sunk her teeth into his arm and kicked, clawing him with her back legs. Head jerked back and forth to cause as much damage as possible.

Lyric was dropped back onto the floor and she groaned while she tried to get her arms under herself. If only she had magic like she once used to. Then she could at least call to the Earth and use it to restrain the vengeful and angry once-god in the room. Or kill him.

The sound of voices outside got her attention and she turned towards the broken window right until she heard a yelp of Asteri being flung off. She just barely managed to push herself up to catch the dog and scrambled towards a wall. Trying to put distance between herself and Stephen as he pursued her. Asteri whined and tried to snarl in warning at the male.

"Lyric!" The voice belonged to James as he rushed to her side. Right behind him was a giant man who immediately saw Stephen and blocked the man from them. The large man instead grabbed Stephen's neck and, with nothing but a soft grunt from effort, slammed the man into the floor like a doll.

James gave a thin smile to the giant before looking over Lyric with concern. His eyes were glassy from disorientation and his forehead head bled from where something had struck him, "Where is Lord Had- Tahvo?"

"Over there. I don't know if he…" She trailed off. Her voice cracked at the very thought of him dead. Lyric didn't know if he survived that. Vision started to blur, "I need to make sure he is okay. I don't want him to die. He was sick and…"

"I'll get you to him." James told her with soothing tones. A careful move to scoop her up and carry her, focusing on the placement of his feet. As soon as he set her down, he watched her check his breathing while he checked for a pulse. It was slow and almost seemed sporadic every time his body shook.

"I felt like I was being crushed…. My chest and heart… I don't know if he will…"

"The boss is as old as dirt, My Queen. Probably just has a lot of memories to sift through. Compared to him, I just had a few centuries worth of rowing a boat. Nothing too exciting. At least this life around, I actually remember leg day." He gave a grim smile as he tried to soften her panic with his humor. Though his own head throbbed.

While Lyric was glad that James remembered things as well, it did not ease her panic. So he was Charon? It had been far too long since she had spoken to any of them, "We need to call the police. Also we need to get Pandora's box from Stephen."

A thin smile and she looked over at the man pinning Stephen, "So, is that Marco? Is he one of ours or just one of the mortals?"

"The minotaur." James said as casually as possible. While James had been the one driving when the memories hit, it puzzled him that Marco had not suffered much disorientation. Perhaps it was simply the lifespan. He seemed amused at her surprised look as he looked over at the door where Spot was sprawled on the floor, "We called when we saw smoke. So someone should be here soon. Though on perhaps a random note, I really need to ask Tahvo how he decided on Spot's pedigree name."

"Perhaps because of the dreams." Lyric told him. After checking Tahvo one more time, she crawled across the floor to the black hound. Her arms still cradled Asteri against her chest. The dog in her arms might have been the only normal soul there.

"You've been a very good boy, Cerberus. Both you and Asteri were very brave today. Thank you so much." She scratched and pet them both while she tried to regain some semblance of strength. Lyric wasn't entirely sure why she was able to function at all. Maybe it was her fear of Stephen permanently hurting Tahvo.

She wished Tahvo was awake. It would do wonders to ease her worry, but she knew he had not felt well before this. Hell, he had put a lot of himself and his magic into making the spell that locked all of the memories and the power the pantheon into Pandora's Box. Unlocking it was probably just as exhausting, and that hadn't been a willing act.

James gave a thin smile at the woman who had once been his Queen before glancing down at Tahvo. He watched as a shudder rocked the crumpled male. While Charon had barely known Hades beyond anything professional, in this life he had gotten to know Tahvo well. The life his boss had given them all was considerably far more pleasant in comparison. Especially if the few people he had déjà vu with were the people he thought they were.

"Thank you again, James. You seem to have been saving me a lot lately." Lyric said.

She took a deep breath and pet both dogs to soothe them until she heard sirens. The flashing lights grew brighter as the sounds got louder as they came up the drive. Marco dropped the now unconscious Stephen and stepped back. He tucked the tiny black box high on the shelf and then prepared to sit on his knees. Just in time for officers to shout outside for everyone to have their hands in the air.

Everyone complied as the officers stormed in and took in the mess of a living room. The two unconscious men were noted first and the group split as the vitals of the two were checked. Most of them were uuneasy about Marco watching them with a blank look, complying with every-thing he was asked to do. As they checked and called for ambulances, the questions as to what happened started coming.

Lyric omitted the fun supernatural stuff in exchange for *most* of the truth. Which was how Stephen had forced his way through the window when she refused to answer the door. The fire which was clearly evident with the scorched walls, curtain, ceiling, and her hands. The assault on her and Tahvo's person and the rescue by James and Marco. Given she had made a previous complaint about Stephen, they had no real problem making sure his ambulance came with police escort.

The ambulances got there and they gave them the information as to which hospital Tahvo and Stephen would be taken. Lyric refused a ride and promised to follow after. James promised to take her there and they were soon zipping off after the ambulances with their own police escort as to keep up.

Lyric sat in the back while James drove. Marco merely hummed something oddly soothing. She swore it was some jazz music. She noticed he was very quiet. Then again, knowing who he was, his memories had to have been incredibly unpleasant. Smashing Zeus into the floor had probably brought him so much pleasure, although she knew Poseidon was definitely going to have it coming.

When they got there, Lyric was pretty sure the staff at the front desk went into a panic upon seeing her. Though she spoke up quickly to tell them who she was looking for. They still demanded to check her in, making the woman sigh good naturedly. A smile at the two men who drove her there, "You two should go and get some rest. I promise to call you when he wakes up. Can you go back to the house and make sure the dogs are okay? There are puppies and a cat there too an-"

"I know what is there, Lyric." James smiled at her starting to fret like Tahvo always did over the animals. They were a good match for one another, "I will make sure to get everyone cared for. Go get checked. Clean up so that Tahvo can wake to seeing you whole and alive."

Lyric nodded and hugged them both tightly, "Thank you both so much. Seriously, I owe you dinner when we are done. You come over and I will make the best food. I bet if you bring some drinks over, we can make a party of it." James hugged her back lightly. Marco seemed startled that she hugged him without an ounce of fear and gently hugged her back before she followed a nurse back to the room Tahvo was in. Thankfully there was a second bed in there. One miraculously available for her.

Somehow, Lyric had not suffered too horrible of injuries. Just a bit of bruising and cuts and the worst was probably the burns on her hands. Her hair probably needed cut now. Eyes drifted constantly to the male unconscious on the bed. The IV drip in his arm a mix of saline and medications. One of the nurses urged her to go take advantage of the hospital showers. That if he woke up, they would make sure she knew.

Lyric wasn't sure if she felt disappointed or not that he was still unconscious when she got back. Her clothes smelled too much of smoke and brought on too many horrible memories, but the hospital gown was awful and drafty. It made her huddle with blankets wrapped tightly around her as she curled on a chair right beside his bed. With a towel wrapped around her hair, she rested her head against his bed. Deciding that the cold was worth it, she stuck her hand out of her blanket cocoon and grasped one of his hands. Eyes studying his split knuckles.

"I remember you, my Love. I remember everything now." She whispered to him.

"I remember the way you smiled at me when I first kissed you. I remember every time you laughed when we were alone. Even the times we were not, I remember the way your face turned red when you realized everyone else heard you." She gently kissed his knuckles. Eyes closed as she did so.

"I remember the fury you held for Zeus. How afraid I was of you when I found out and... the way you held me and promised me that you didn't blame me for what Zeus did to me. The way you held me close when I had Zagreus. The way you played with him every day as if he were yours. I remember what pushed us to finally tear the pantheon down." Zeus hadn't wanted *his* son to be 'tainted' with too much of the underworld. So he had taken the child away to Olympus. Away from her when his wretched wife had her child killed by Titans.

"I was so scared when you first told me your plan. Yet you had left it up to me. That scared me too. What if I made the wrong decision? Yet... I don't feel like I did now. I miss knowing the people I did then, but I am so glad I got to live this life too. I've met so many people. I've done so many new things and I finally found you again."

Lyric was so glad she had found her Hades again. Hells, she even initiated the first date between them. Even without knowing who he was, she had wanted to stay with him. He made her happy and safe. His smile brought her comfort and he did what he could to offer her a freedom of choice. The fact that he could be in the sunlight and make friends was entirely worth it to her. He could care for the living instead of the dead.

"I want to learn you all over again, Tahvo. I want Lyric to learn and love her Tahvo just as Persephone loved her Hades. You did it right this time around." She assured his unconscious form, "You even kept Stephen from doing something terrible to me all over again. Thank you."

Tahvo shifted very slightly as if that roused him, causing her to look up suddenly and see a peek of eyes looking down at her and their hands. The woman didn't move right away as she let him draw his hand from hers and touch her cheek.

"You should have been a muse." He murmured.

Lyric found her cheeks going red hot as she stared at the sleeping form. Joy of his consciousness mixing with embarrassment, "How long have you been awake?"

"Somewhere around 'loved her Hades' I think. Brain is a bit fuzzy around the edges. I am *old*." He lamented quietly and then added. "Are you alright?"

"Yes, just a bit sore and bruised, but I am okay. Head hurt for a while until the pain meds kicked in." She couldn't help but smile up at him. A lean into his hand and curled her fingers around his, "I was so afraid you weren't going to wake up."

In all honesty, Tahvo had been afraid too. Eyes closed as he took several deep breaths while a stab of a migraine hit. Definitely was going to ask for pain medicine when he could, "How are the animals?"

He would be the one to ask about the animals before anything else, "Cerberus is a bit sore, but good. I think Asteri is just a bit stunned and sore. James and Marco are making sure everyone is alright."

"Good." He closed his eyes and frowned, "Pain medication and food. I am willing to bet their kitchen is closed. Think you could bribe James into bring us something to eat? I only got a few bites of dinner before things went insane."

Lyric nodded and smiled, "I am sure if we gave him two cents, he will happily bring it to us. Only if we pay him after though." Watching Tahvo work through her words made her all too pleased as he realized the joke she made.

"That was terrible, my Queen. Perhaps for that we can just order take out." He groaned at her, but there was still a smile upon his lips.

"Well, I have a few millennia worth of really bad jokes to make." She grinned at him impishly before slowly uncurling from her chair, "I'll go tell the doctor you are awake so they can get you medicine. I have to call James and Marco anyway. I will order some food." A lean down to kiss his cheek. Eyes closing as she listened to his waking breaths. Hopefully he could manage to stay awake for a bit longer.

Tahvo nodded and gently let his hand drop from her face. Watching as she shuffled out of the room. The sight was actually rather amusing given she looked like a little blanket burrito. He was still sifting through most of his memories, but it was hard when he felt so weak. The migraine in his head was not helping by any means. Lyric's return to the room came with a doctor and a lot of questions as he was examined. As well as the go ahead for food. Tahvo tiredly thanked the doctor as she went off to get some pain medication. While he hurt, he was glad he wasn't all alone in the room.

Though a single question continued to nag at him: What next?

7

"HADES!" A voice echoed through all of the Underworld in a thundering echo. One that made the very stone tremble at the fury of one so dangerous. The voice belonged to Persephone.

*Hades had been busy trying to deal with the trouble at hand. That was, he was verbally tearing into the goddess Hera. The titans had no other reason to do something so incredibly stupid as to hurt **his** son. Yet they had. Persephone had gone to talk to Zeus and plea to have him save their child.*

*"You will never bring harm unto mine again, you wretched cow." Hades hissed to Hera and watched her become offended. Which he frankly did not care, "Remember whose hands you will be in when your end finds you. I will **not** be kind. Now leave!"*

"Hades!" Persephone yelled again and he turned as soon as he cast the rotten bitch out from his realm. He saw the red eyes and fury with every step. Curls of deadly

magic seeping from every step and causing the very stone underfoot to ripple like water.

"What has happened, Persephone? Has he refused to aide us?" He would 'speak' to Zeus himself if needed. He felt Persephone burrow into his chest and she shook from anger.

The goddess tried to calm herself before she tried to go toe to toe with the god of the sky, "He adhered my... all that was left was his heart! He adhered it to his **hip** like some sort of tumor! Told me that it was best that the child was raised away from the darkness. That if I had been a better...." That none of it would have happened.

Persephone could not hold back as she tilted her head back and screamed. Pain and grief rattled the realm as her heartbreak came from somewhere deep. True love had been given to the child and it had been shattered. Labored breaths escaped her as she tried to calm down. The goddess started to pace as she didn't want to harm her husband. He did not cause any of this.

"Your plans! We must begin your plans!" Persephone demanded as she drew back. Then she took a deep breath and rubbed at her face, "I will not allow Zeus to twist that child into a monster. My son will not be reborn to a selfish beast such as him!"

Hades stared at his wife. For only her sake the god had not gone forward with plans made from anger. Instead *he watched her ready to tear the pantheon apart, with or without their plan. He was furious too, but he knew her fury far surpassed his own. She poured so much love into the child she had thought was his and now that was ruined. The god bowed deeply and looked into her eyes with a solemn expression, "You know what you ask of me. Do you permit turn us down this path?"*

"Just tell me what you need of me, husband mine. They will know the wrath of Persephone, Queen of Hades!" The goddess stepped forward and looked into his eyes with an unwavering determination.

"As you wish."

Lyric was more than happy when James came to the rescue and brought food. Not only that, but James had arrived as soon as he received the call that Tahvo had woken up and brought a couple of thick blankets as well so they wouldn't freeze. He even brought her bag of clothes from Tahvo's house. By the time they finished eating, Tahvo looked so much better than before. It brought relief.

It was entertaining for Lyric to watch Tahvo give detailed instructions and needs for every animal. James took it in stride as his boss' tone changed and the form of address went from being simply James to Mr. Cheroni. Lyric swore that if she hadn't known better, that Tahvo was an entirely different person. There was no stuttering and jumping in surprise. Just a surety in the man that knew exactly what he wanted from people around him.

Working with the living certainly suited him far better. Given Hades had known already how to manage such a large number of souls, she was glad to see he learned to delegate the large numbers of animals to others he learned to trust. One had to imagine how hard it was to find people he was comfortable with and trusted. Probably looked for people who *knew* the field. Knew more than enough about the animals they all helped care for.

Oh, but her heart broke when his eyes flashed in anger instead of content. James told them what happened to the missing horse. That calm turned into a silent fury that stormed into his eyes. An anger that she felt must have been drawn on when Tahvo had come in to stop his brother from harming her further. So very badly did she just want to wrap him in her arms to chase the pain and fury away. Instead she settled with the fact that all three of them discussed a way to make a small memorial to the lost horse.

When all other subjects were settled, Tahvo told James to get home and finally go back to sleep. By tomorrow, he hoped to be home and taking care of the clinic and grounds himself. A sincere thanks and Tahvo's demeanor finally seemed to relax when they were alone again. He studied Lyric and realized he was unsure about how to address topics that came to mind now. After all, the pair had history and Tahvo wasn't sure where to go from there.

When he looked down at his hands, he finally spoke, "What do we do now? I mean, ah, about us? Do we treat things as we used to back then or do we pretend we didn't just get our memories back?"

What *were* they supposed to do? Lyric frowned as she thought about it. A shift to sit on the edge of his bed so that one of her hands could gently take his. Fingers weaving with his as she realized she wasn't entirely sure either. She knew that her hand fit with his well. That he gave her a sense of calm and yet lit a fire in her soul that made her want to run out into the world and make it hers. Of course, there was a huge potential of more people becoming terrifying and violent just like Stephen had. People who didn't want to be ripped from their godhood and would take it upon themselves to claim their revenge. How many more attempts on their lives would there be now?

"Well, we can't exactly shove the cat back in the bag. It is free and knocking all of the glasses off the tables. Could always treat it like... um..." She thought hard, brows scrunched together as she rested her chin on her other hand, "Like a couple of kids who dated in high school! We just happened to go separate ways and happened to meet up again."

Tahvo snorted in abrupt laughter, "We would have been awful in high school. The things we've done together..."

They were so not things that were ever high school appropriate. Those long ago memories made him want to pull the woman closer to him, he managed to refrain barely.

"Well, we did essentially 'burn' the metaphorical school down." Lyric mused with a smile. Her eyes slowly looked over him. Some of the memories of the far more pleasurable activities made her heart race and her cheeks feel just a little warmer, "Not that I would terribly mind a reenactment. I recall some very interesting things we have done with magic. It certainly would be a fun activity for if I move in with you." Her words were a soft purr as she leaned in and kissed his cheek.

Now it was Tahvo's turn for his face to become warm. He shifted the way his legs were under the covers so that his... excitement was not so blatantly obvious. As if he hadn't already started having those kinds of thoughts when he kissed her for the first time. Now there were memories to back it and a curiosity for if her sounds would be just as intoxicating this time around.

"That sounds, ah, delightful. Although..." He felt a tiny bit of doubt crawl into his chest, "Do you think you would even want to move in after all of this? I would not wish to endanger you with choices I have made." Was his voice too hopeful? Did it make him pathetic if he was? While he, rather, while Hades knew Persephone intimately, he did not know Lyric nearly to that degree. Lyric was someone with her very own experiences, thoughts, and feelings separate from her life as Persephone. To ignore the potential that she could very well not love him as much as Persephone had loved Hades would be foolish.

"Well, I had thought about it all day when I was at work. Someone has to make sure you remember to eat after all." It was also a matter of not wanting to be away from him again. Hades or not, Tahvo had made her feel safe thus far. He supported her freedom and seemed very determined to continue to do so.

Tahvo lit up at her response and he couldn't have stopped his smile, "Well, someone needs to make sure you eat as well. How do you want to tell your mother? Do you need me to come with you?"

Gods... she forgot about her mother, "I don't need her assaulting you too. She is already going to screech. Despite the fact that I love the work the shop has given me, I would rather have one of my own. Plus, I have a lot of land I need to care for when it comes to the clinic. I imagine that will keep me pretty busy for a while. I don't care what she does, Tahvo. I have a choice and I choose to learn everything about *this* version of you."

"I suppose it would be very labor intensive. I would like to make a memorial. I have one with plaques on one of the outside walls of the clinic. But I would like something more... prominent and lively if we can, Ms. Helios." He then realized he went into work mode again and blushed, ducking his head a little to hide it with his hair, "Ah, sorry, I mean... Lyric."

"It's alright. I think it is very charming when you go into work mode." She smiled sunnily, "And pretty cute too if I am being absolutely honest." Which Lyric never could find it in herself to truly fib. Especially not to him.

Her gaze met his and held him with the intensity of her gaze, "And while I am being absolutely honest with you. I have so much time I want to make up for. I have a chance to choose you again and in this life I won't give it up easily."

Tahvo's heart raced as she spoke. Gods, this passion was exactly why Hades loved her as Persephone. The depth of passion and conviction in her was belied by her words. The woman would do whatever she set out to do. When her mind was made up, not a thing could stop her. Her name became a whisper of a storm that was fierce when invoked.

"I want to as well, my Winter Jewel." Tahvo whispered the words of the pet name he once reserved for important moments. With their hands still intertwined, he used that to yank her to him and caused her to spill onto his lap. His other hand moved carefully with the needles and tubes still in it to cup her lower back. With that bit of effort, Tahvo pulled her close so that they could kiss.

When Lyric realized what he intended to do, she helped by moving her free hand to cup the back of his neck. Lips claimed his with a ferocity she hadn't realized she felt. That drive to feel him alive and well, Somehow the weight of their memories just made it that much more pertinent.

Lyric needed to let him know with actions that she wanted this new life with him to work out.

Despite the fact that it would be an absolutely horrible idea, Tahvo was tempted to pull his IV out. However, he refrained and instead kissed back with just as much fervor. Fingers kneaded Lyric's lower back as he leaned back on the bed. His kisses began to make a hot trail down along her jaw line and towards her ear when someone cleared their throat.

Both froze and looked over slowly at the red-faced nurse standing at the doorway. Both of them became just as red. Lyric quickly drew away and perched at the edge of the bed, a soft apology escaping as she tried clearing her throat. Her hand moved to ruffle her own hair and try to hide her face. Geeze, they *were* acting like a pair of love-sick teenagers again. Gods help them, they were going to end up misbehaving in the middle of the street at this rate. Not that the idea was unappealing, but jail-cells tended to be.

"Sorry to, um, disturb you." The nurse said softly. Her name was Daphne. A very sweet woman that had been helping the pair while they were there. Poor thing was probably traumatized now, "I wanted to let you know that the police would be up here shortly to speak to you both." She then took a step back. Unsure if they needed anything or not, but too embarrassed to try and figure out how to use her words.

Tahvo managed to save the day, "Thank you, Daphne." Look, he even did it without his voice cracking in embarrassment! The nurse seemed relieved at the unsaid dismissal and scurried out. When the two were alone again, Tahvo looked over at Lyric who was in a sudden fit of helpless giggles. A smirk tugged at his lips as he watched her totally lose it.

"You know, Lyric, some people enjoy being an exhibitionist." He gently tugged her back enough to be able to trace his fingers along the line of her jaw. Just ever so slightly grazing her throat with his nails. That answering shudder that scattered her giggled emboldened him to continue with slow sensuous circles along bared skin.

"Well..." She swallowed at the thought. The idea of being caught mid-coitus was nearly exhilarating. Self-preservation was winning by a small margin though, "Being in front of people isn't too terrible. Being arrested isn't that pleasant though. I don't think it is good conduct and pretty sure they would panic at your heartrate getting a little too high."

Oh gods, the things Lyric could do to him with the look he was giving her right now. The things she *wanted* to do to him. Things that would get them into so much trouble. Her need to feel his skin entirely against her own. Lips against her skin again. She wished that the touch by his fingers, almost scorching hot as they were now, would run against her sides instead. Her imagination was trying to run wild and it was getting hard to remember why they wanted to behave.

"Mm, too bad." He purred as he dropped his hand just a little lower. Tahvo's knuckles brushed teasingly across the perk nipple that showed through the hospital gown. That elicited a soft sound as her back arched, "Imagine the eyeful we could have given that nurse."

Any response Lyric would have given to that was interrupted with a sharp rapping on the door. Lyric blinked dazed as Tahvo drew his hands back from her. It allowed her to retreat into the safety of the chair. Safe for everyone else at least, given she just nearly had wanted to peel every shred of clothing off of the male in the bed.

"Come in!" Lyric called instead.

The door opened with a solemn looking officer entering. He looked over them with a frown. That pensive look in his eyes set the two in the room on edge. That they dreaded such a look was over something they did not truly wish to think about.

"Do either of you have somewhere else to stay?" The offer asked as lightly as he could. Which didn't seem to help at all when Lyric looked immediately alarmed. The strength of such a reaction was not one he expected as she shot up stick straight like a frightened cat.

"Stephen vanished again didn't he?" Lyric asked. When the officer nodded, panic filled her. It was the same as last time too. He had vanished without a trace and then there was fire. She shivered, "I don't think... that is the clinic cannot just be left alone. We can take precautions."

"We will have to." Tahvo added. It pained him to be unable to chase away her panic, "We can't leave the animals. Thank you for telling us, Officer. Unfortunately, I cannot check on the clinic from here. Until we are cleared, could you please send someone down to check on the house and clinic? I have been made recently aware of my brother's penchant for arson. Aside from the normal breaking and entering."

"We can do that, Doctor. I hope you both recover quickly." The officer promised. With that, he gave them both his contact information and left.

An uncomfortable silence filled the room as Lyric pulled her legs up to her chest. The blanket she had been using was tucked around her. Eyes closed tightly as she tried to swallow the fear bubbling up in her chest. Stephen... Zeus had been absolutely murderous. He was so determined to make sure they knew why he wanted to kill them both. That he wanted to hurt them as much as possible before he did so. Maybe they deserved it.

Tahvo shifted in the bed and reached out to her, "Lyric." He said her name sternly to get her to look at him. Then his voice became soft, "Come here please."

Lyric blinked at him with a deer-in-headlights expression. Finally, she moved and crawled onto his bed. He scooted over to give her space and rolled to lay on his side so that he could pull her close. Nothing like of he was doing with her moments ago. Just a comforting hold while he kissed her forehead, "I won't let him hurt you again, Lyric."

Lyric shuddered and then looked at him, eyes wide and afraid, "It isn't me I am afraid of him hurting. When he was standing over you today..." Her voice was pitched and she sounded so small. A terrifying thought ripped through her, "What if he still has powers? He had his memories, he could somehow have those too. What if he goes after James and Marco and.... Oh gods, Tahvo even though my mother upsets me, I don't want her dead either." Her voice cracked as she went onto a panicked tangent.

He could just kill Stephen for the way he made her afraid. Tahvo wasn't about to tell her there was no reason to be afraid at all. It was a legitimate fear, "How about you call James and Marco first. Then call your mother. Put them on alert. After that, we should get rest. The sooner we rest, the more likely we will get out of here and home tomorrow. We can even stop by your mother's so you can see that she is alive and well."

She nodded numbly and fumbled around until she got the hospital phone. Lyric called a very tired Marco and James. Assured the two would be safe, Lyric stared at the phone as she hesitated in her next call. Gods, did she really not want to speak to her mother over the phone. The hospital phone even.

"If she starts screeching, cover your ears. She might bust an eardrum." Lyric sighed and then worked on dialing. Snuggling up against Tahvo, she closed her eyes and listened to the dial tone. Then she heard a snappy 'what' over the phone. Well, she did just wake up her mother from sleeping. Dear gods help her with this phone call.

"Hey Mom, it's me." She began. Before she could continue the voice snapped back.

"Why the hell are you calling so late?!" Lyric assumed that her mother probably hadn't bothered to check the caller I.D. Not sure if that was a good thing or not.

"Well, Stephen came back a couple nights ago. He attacked me at the apartment. I spent the night at Tahvo's to be safe-"

"I thought I said to stay away from him!" Dinara shouted her voice making Lyric draw the phone away from her ear. Then dead silence hung heavy in the air and she whispered, "Kore?"

Lyric nearly dropped the phone. Was that her.... She stared at the phone and her voice went soft, "Zeus tried to kill me. I don't know if he is after you too. I'll talk to you later. Goodnight, Mother." She didn't want to talk anymore. She hung up the phone fast and shoved it away.

"What's wrong?" Tahvo asked softly. Hand carefully smoothed her hair out. He was going to take her somewhere to get her hair trimmed so the burnt bits weren't still there. He watched her stare up at him. Those golden eyes bright and scared. Confusion was the dominating factor as well.

"My mother is Demeter."

8

Lyric sat in Tahvo's car and stared at the shop front of the plant nursery. Tahvo was sitting beside her. Frankly, neither wanted to be there. Yet here they were. It was a beast of a problem they had to tackle. If only it would solve itself, but life was never that simple.

"Are you sure you want to come with me? Mom was cranky before when we all thought we were human. At this rate she will be incandescent now."

"I don't want to make you face her alone. I have long been used to Demeter's ah... moods. I am sure Dinara won't be as much trouble as my brother." Tahvo assured her softly. He unbuckled his belt and leaned over to kiss her cheek. Both of them were still drained from yesterday's events. Even so, they didn't need more nonsense smashing angrily through the windows of the house or the clinic. Nor more fire.

"Our luck, she'll try stabbing you with a trowel." Lyric mumbled. His kiss eased her fears only a little. Though she seriously was half expecting them to need another trip to the hospital. Demeter's and Dinara's personalities and temper were a volatile combination.

Tahvo snorted. Demeter would have done that back then too. Though she used a much sharper implement back then to stab him. Luckily, she didn't carry one of the random god killing kinds. Bah, they were just finding more reasons to stall. Finally, he worked up the nerve to open his door rounding about the vehicle to help Lyric out. The car locked with a click and for a moment, things were all too silent. Then Lyric straightened her back and started walking. Tahvo stayed close to her as they approached the building. It was good he had because after a few steps Lyric clutched his hand.

While she didn't openly voice her fear, he could feel her shaking. The longer she held his hand though, the less she trembled. He smiled inwardly at her bravery for the situation. In that moment he was proud of her and he hoped that alone could give her the confidence to push forward.

They stepped into the shop and it was quiet. Tahvo looked around the shop. Walls covered in shelves full of various plants, pots, and little balloons. One part looked like it had various lawn decorations. The statues looked rather nice and part of him wanted to venture off to take in the whole shop. It had looked so big on the outside, but inside with everything bustling with greenery and blooms, it was like a dense forest. He idly reached for the leaf of a vined plant to touch it when someone spoke.

"Get him out of here." The demanding voice was low and angry. The pale haired woman came out from the back and glared at Tahvo. Then she looked at Lyric with a deep frown, "You are late *again*. You have a mountain of deliv- erie-"

"I've been in the hospital! I was assaulted!" Lyric shouted, absolutely disgusted with the heartlessness of her mother. She held up her wrist that still had the medical band on it. A tight squeeze of Tahvo's hand to make sure he didn't leave her before she spoke again. "I was almost killed!"

"Well, being killed certainly hadn't bothered you the first time around, now did it, Kore?" Dinara snapped loudly at her. A glare up at Tahvo and then sneered, "Hades. I should have known you would find some way to try and take my daughter away from me *again*. Get your hands off *my* daughter and get out of *my* shop!"

Tahvo could not help but pin her with a glare, "I believe she goes by the name of Lyric now. She has disowned the name Kore for a long time. I think it would be disrespectful to continue calling her that. If you must call her anything else, then the only other alternative is Persephone." Then a shake of his head, "I am not leaving unless my queen tells me to. As she has not yet sent me away, I am currently going to remain, Ms Dinara."

Lyric looked up at him and chanced a small smile at him. Though with the way his hand twitched in hers, she could tell it was taking so much out of him. They needed to get home. Instead of showing her mother that Tahvo was on the edge of being anything but calm, she instead looked apologetically at her mother,

"I'm sorry for my choices, Mother. After Zeus seduced me like he had so many other people, I barely could stand my own existence. When he took Zagreus away after Hera..." She paused, that particular memory fresh and painful, "I couldn't live that way anymore. I already had to spend so much time away from Hades. To lose my son before he was even..."

"Yet you continue to try and leave *me*." Dinara snapped. "You are my only daughter and yet you chose some man over your own mother. They are all the same, Kore. They only have ever wanted only one thing from us."

"Mother, please! You have raised me from childhood and up twice now! More than I have ever been able to do for my own child! You need to let me go. I promise to still pay back everything to you, even the new shop, but I am not going to work here anymore. Not if you are going to make it feel like a cruel cage." The place she loved to work and help at as a child had become an unpleasant chore. A pretty prison that she had no escape from.

Dinara glared and stepped forward, "Oh, and you do recall our agreement? Where are you going to live? With *him*?"

"That is for me to worry about. You never were terribly worried before. So long as I was still paying you, that is what mattered right?" Lyric shook her head in disappointment. She started to pull Tahvo along with her, "You can keep everything from my apartment. Since that counts towards assets. I will make sure you get paid back in full."

Dinara moved fast, placing herself between the pair and the door, "You are not going anywhere."

Lyric frowned at her mother and tried to find a path around her. Suddenly her free hand was grabbed and she was yanked hard away from Tahvo. A sound of pain escaped as she tried to dig her heels in. Being grabbed like that instantly sent her mind into a panic, reminding her why she hated when her mother did it.

All panic seemed to die when Tahvo stepped forward and gripped Dinara's wrist in a way that caused her hand to go slack. It wasn't hard, but it was enough to make the silence in the shop loud. Fierce eyes stared at him in astonishment. Lyric was staring at him too, drawing her arm back to her chest and cradling it and hiding the new bruises slowly blooming from the force her mother used.

"You will no longer assault your daughter nor trap her. Your daughter is not a prisoner for you to keep. I did this so that she could *choose* to come and go through the world as she pleased. So that she could decide who she wishes to spend her life with without being prisoner to the Underworld *or you*." His voice dropped into a low growl, "And if you seek to continue to try and trap her, I will not hesitate to ensure you can never undo the work I have done to ensure her chance at freedom."

"You are threatening to hurt me, Hades?"

"Tahvo." He corrected her flatly, "And I will not harm you, even if you have given me a multitude of reasons to do so. I know plenty of lawyers, Dinara. They would make you whimper and run with their tail tucked between their legs. Do not forget, I was the one who granted haven in the fields or misery in Tartarus." He stepped forward enough to stand between Dinara and Lyric ensuring the stunned woman's hand was still in his grasp, "I came with her so that she could have a civil conversation with you. *Do not dare* harm Lyric in such a manner again else the next time I may forget myself and I will not be so gentle."

Tahvo angry was astonishing, but also terrifying to watch. It wasn't a destructive anger so much as a cool fury. A protective streak in him that crawled up and out any time it seemed those he cared for were in danger even while he had served as Hades instead of the mortal he was now. His body was tense as he stepped out of the way. Just close enough to intervene again if needed after releasing Dinara's wrist. He let Lyric stand on her own facing her mother.

"Look, Mother, I love you. Truly. It was why I called last night. I don't want you hurt." Lyric told her softly. Would it be easier if she actually hated her mother? Not really. Despite the way her mother treated her as she became older, as a child she had given her love in. Given her a home. It was difficult to ignore that.

Years of care did not absolve her of her actions though. Maybe that was the mistake Lyric kept making now. She kept hoping something would change. For some reason she still stayed, despite wanting to work so hard to get out and get away. Maybe it made her broken. Hope had twisted everything and had begun to make her bitter to the world. Lyric was not entirely sure how she felt now, but she felt her heart break just the same as her mother glared at her. As she was looked upon as though she were a disappointment of the very Earth they stood upon.

"Expect a call from my attorney then. I still expect restitution for all you have cost me, Miss Helios." Dinara took on a cold tone as she straightened her back. Glaring at both of them, she added, "Get out of my store."

"Mo-" Lyric started weakly. Never did she want her mother to hate her. Instead of finishing her sentence, she flinched when Dinara took a step towards her with a hand raised. With words dead on her lips, her mother then froze when Tahvo stepped forward. There was another moment of eternal stillness before the hand then pointed at the door. A soundless order for them to leave.

Tahvo gently took Lyric's hand to gently draw her out of stillness. Placing himself protectively between the two. Guilt gnawed at his heart. Had his involvement worsened things? Probably, but he couldn't have just abandoned her to this. Though he suspected nothing about the relationship between the two was healthy. Not that his familiar relationships had faired any better. They managed a few steps before Lyric stopped and looked back helplessly at her mother. Tears formed in her eyes and blurred her vision.

"Please be safe, Mother."

"Address me as Ms. Gallan from now on. For I have no daughter." Her words seemed to make the entire room colder. One could almost claim to have seen the plants begin to wilt.

Tahvo suppressed a shiver and looked down at Lyric and urged her to walk again. Soft words murmured as he could see her begin to cry. He wanted to protect her from further pain. By the time they got to the door, Lyric sniffed quietly and then straightened her back. Glassy eyes betrayed the strength she pretended to have. Tears fell, but she still slipped her hand from Tahvo's to push the door open and walk out with her head held high.

They walked to his car in silence and climbed in. Tahvo wasn't entirely sure what to say to Lyric who seemed more intent on staring out the window than speaking. Instead of pushing, he simply drove them home. After several minutes he finally was able to raise his voice through the heavy silence.

"I apologize for anything I did to make things worse."

Lyric shook her head at him, hand wiping at her eyes. She let out a little sniff. The woman was afraid to speak. If she tried, she was certain all that would come out would be a horrible sob. As it stood, she barely kept her tears in check. Some slipped out, but it didn't hinder her ability to see just yet.

By the time they got home, they could see James' car in the drive. When they pulled into the garage and the ignition switched off, they sat silently where the only sounds were the car settling.

"Do you think I did the right thing?" Lyric asked softly. Her voice cracking and she gave a sniff. Vision blurred. Hands trembled as she looked at him, entirely lost.

How was he supposed to answer that tactfully? Tahvo felt like he was floundering as he very carefully reached out to take one of her hands. How he wished he could chase her pain away so it could never haunt her again. Instead, he leaned forward to kiss a tear from her cheek.

"I cannot promise it will be the right answer I am giving you, but I do think you had made the right choice to distance yourself from her physically." He screwed up his face. That didn't seem to come out right. He tried again, "I mean... I understand that she is your mother. So you will still love her because of that. I don't think you are wrong in that, but until you are ready, it might be good to have space. She must allow you to make your own decisions."

Lyric nodded at him numbly and blinked away tears, "I don't feel like I know how to be my own person. I've spent so much of my life doing everything that I knew pissed my mother off. I mean, I did it because I wanted to, but I also did it to annoy her."

"Well, I think that is a thing all children do at some point. Sometimes we like to get under the skin of our parents. I may have been well behaved compared to Stephen, but I was still a bit of a brat. Though I displayed it in a different way. Sarcasm is a hell of a defense mechanism."

He was sarcastic? It was hard to imagine Tahvo being sarcastic when he seemed very plain spoken. No one could question if he actually meant something or not. The thought was enough to momentarily distract her from how upset she was, "I find it hard to believe you were ever sarcastic."

"Well, I did eventually exchange it for being dry and literal." Tahvo admitted, "But sometimes it slips out and suddenly I am telling my horses 'Yes, please throw me off again. I love the feel of testing gravity in the morning.'" He offered her a faint smile as his sarcasm had been delivered with a seamless change of tone.

Well then, when he said it that way, it was hard not to be amused. A tearful giggle and she sniffed again. Wiping at her eyes, she shifted in her seat to lean against him. Oh, she loved her mother, truly. It killed her to hear her mother disown her. Hopefully her mother would come to her senses soon before the bridge between them crashed down after it was set ablaze.

They sat like that for a few minutes, Tahvo held her against him as best he could in the car. Feeling her slowly fall apart as sniffles turned into quiet sobs. Comforting strokes from his hand over her hair and shoulder. Tahvo wished he could tell her that for absolute certain she had done the right thing. He felt she did the best she could for herself, but as to if it was right or not? When he could see her hurting so badly, it was hard for it to feel like the *right* solution to her problem. It was difficult to feel confident in his proximity to her not being a cause of endless misery.

Then again, sometimes the right thing was the most painful. At least that is what he thought could be the case. He blinked as he looked over to the window where Marco was standing. The giant was bent down oddly after he tapped the glass. Concern in his eyes as he looked in at them both through the window. Tahvo shifted enough to unlock the door and motioned for Marco to open it.

The silent giant did and peered in at Lyric and Tahvo, "Did Zeus harm you again?" His voice was deep and graveled as though the answer could make him snarl like a beast at any moment. Yet instead Marco remained calm, as though doing it for the sake of the woman crying in the car.

Lyric blinked and looked at Marco. She wiped at her face and shook her head, "No, just dealing with my mo-." She choked off at the word with a soft sob.

Marco nodded knowingly and dug into his back pocket and held a small mangled pack of travel tissues and held it out to her. He watched her take it from him carefully. The smile she had forming at trying to uncrinkle it was worth it, "James brought things to make burgers. Would you like us to cook it instead?"

Lyric dabbed at her eyes and face and then blew her nose. It made her feel a little more like a functioning human being. Finally she gave a half-hearted smile, "No, I said I would cook. I promised to feed you all and I need something to do. Thank you, Marco."

He nodded at her and drew back carefully, "I'll tell James then. We had the window fixed too."

Tahvo raised his brow, "How did you get that done so quickly?" Usually it took a bit of work to repair anything, even on short notice. He found curiosity flared when Marco actually gave him a thin smile before leaving. Causing Tahvo to stare after him.

"Well, now I'm curious." Lyric said, blowing her nose again. Gods, she hated crying. Made her feel like her head was a lead balloon. The entire tissue pack was used up and she felt a little better. A hot shower would probably make her feel even better. Then again, so would a hair cut.

Tahvo laughed suddenly, "Ah yes, my Winter Jewel would be curious wouldn't she?" He smiled down at her after using the old pet name. Then he remembered himself and watched to see how she would react as she unbuckled and climbed out of the car. With no adverse reaction he found himself laughing more when she started to amble off. That quickness to her step as she allowed curiosity sweep away her worries to the back of her mind. He followed after her at a slower pace.

When they got into the living room, Cecilia and Orion were sitting and chatting in the living room that looked like absolutely nothing had ever happened to it. Not that it was repaired and cleaned up well. There would have been signs and even the scent of fire and of the work having being done. No, it was as though it had been reset back to how it had been. It was in the air. A familiar itch that the two couldn't quite scratch.

Cecilia heard them both and smiled at Lyric. It had been ages since she had seen her friend. Such a long time ago when they once were playing in a field together before Persephone had been whisked away. Suddenly her friend was living in the underworld for half the year. Her hand raised in a wave, "See, everything is fixed. Animals are safe and behaving just fine."

Tahvo blinked and nodded, trying to place his finger on what the feeling in the room was. Celicia seemed entirely amused by this. Watching his brain flounder with what had been done to clean up and repair everything. Always a pleasure to stump Hades somehow. Especially as she knew the man Hades had become. Still had his nose in his work, but he was softer somehow. The sunlight did some good for him, as did working with the living. Anyone would get grumpy dealing with dead people after a while.

"So, while he is trying to figure out the room, how have you been Lyric? That is what you prefer still for a name, right?" Then the blinked and added, "Oh, I forgot, my name is Cecilia and this is Orion. He is as his name has always been, I was Artemis."

After Cecilia spoke, Lyric blinked and then let out a squeal of joy. Startling all of the men in the room as Lyric dashed and nearly tackled the other woman with a great big hug. She started babbling, consumed with joy

"Oh my gods, Artemis! I mean Cecilia! I haven't seen you in centuries! You found Orion! I am so happy for you!" She hugged her friend tightly until the other gently pried her off. Then Lyric studied at Orion critically. She had never met him properly, but remembered how heartbroken poor Artemis had been every time he was brought up, "I can't believe your parents somehow named you that."

"Apparently any other name ill fit me." Orion gave a mild smile and dipped his head respectfully, "Pleasure to meet you, Lyric. I suppose I should thank you and Tahvo for doing what you had. If you hadn't, I never would have happened to find Lia." He tugged his wife against him with a hug and kissed her cheek. A small moment of warmth and affection. Relief that those who now governed fate had decided to allow him the chance with the goddess of the hunt once more.

A second chance. They had given them a second chance. Lyric couldn't help but smile at them. It had helped more than just herself and Hades, "I am so happy it worked out for you both." Then she looked at the window and frowned a little. She moved around them and ran her fingers along the curtain. It sent a tingling down her arm and she started gaping at it like a fish.

"Magic!" Lyric exclaimed.

"Look at that, she got it before you did, Doctor." Cecilia laughed as she watched Tahvo's eyes widen. Oh this was so totally worth it. Especially as he stared at her and then the curtain and then her, "Yes, oh silent one. I have magic again. You two probably do as well, but I heard someone's been practically starving themselves *again*."

"Hey, I legitimately forget to eat." Tahvo frowned.

"Oh! Food!" Lyric spun from the curtain and started for the kitchen, "James, get out of the kitchen! I told you I owed you guys food and I am going to cook it!" She vanished into the other room, leaving Tahvo in the living room with the couple. Magic. *They had magic again.*

"How did you two realize you had magic?"

"When I came to check on the clinic after we regained our memories. I had a Doctor Dolittle moment. Did you know Muse wants to be a famous author? He wants to write a novel about some guy named Francis. Although apparently bird wings aren't good with keyboards or pencils." Cecilia replied, amused as Tahvo stared at her. He looked as though if he were trying to tell if she was joking or not. If he would have asked, she would have honestly told him that the bird really was serious and so was she.

"I... haven't had anything try talking to me yet. Spot has been rather quiet. Actually..." He frowned. Where was his friend? He was usually up and ready to greet him. Last time he had seen his friend, the dog was barking and snarling at Stephen when the fight broke out. Then there had been pain and... he paled, "Cerberus is alright... isn't he?"

Orion looked over in sympathy and motioned to the stairs, "He was pretty lethargic. I guess James and Marco spent the night here making sure everyone upstairs was good. I think the hound is feeling pretty drained. Don't think dogs were meant to get a headache like that. The little spotted ankle biter is in the kitchen though staring longingly at the burgers."

Tahvo nodded then, "While I really want to figure out the whole magic thing, I need to check on Cerberus first." He then excused himself and quickly went up the stairs. Guilt pulled at him for not having checked on his friend after the hospital.

While he wanted to blame the haze of heavy medication and new memories, he had barely managed to deal with Dinara. Which had led to him threatening the other woman as he reacted poorly to how she treated Lyric. A groan as he rubbed the bridge of his nose. Gods, he was a complete idiot. As he got to his room, he could see those big puppy-like eyes staring at him.

"Hey boy." He said softly as he walked into the room. Tahvo sat on the edge of the bed and pet his best friend. A scratch behind the ear and he leaned down to kiss the top of his head, "Sorry for the headache, buddy. I am so sorry I didn't check on you sooner. I was distracted and stupid. Mostly stupid."

As though forgiving him, Cerberus licked at his face and climbed half-way onto his lap. Tahvo smiled weakly and continued to pet his friend. His nose burned as he felt the pressure in his eyes from tears wanting to fall. The knot forming in his throat hurt as he even had the barest hint of a thought as to what could have happened to his best friend. Cerberus was one of the few companions that kept him constant company in that cold dark place. Despite being a snarly beast to most others, Cerberus was his best friend. If this reincarnation's body had not been able to handle such memories, he could have died. He was not in any sort of state to rescue his friend.

Tahvo wished he could communicate to Cerberus right then like Artemis... Cecilia could. Heck then he could communicate with them all. The ability to understand all tongues, although evolving languages made some wires cross when it came to new words meaning something that was similar but worlds different.

Curling around his friend, he pressed his head against the top of Spot's and hugged him. He could feel the current weakness and drain on his friend's body. The dog was by no means a young puppy. He was old enough that it could have killed him, even if he did act hyper most times.

It would have been all my fault, Tahvo thought. The shock of it all finally shook him and he let out a sob against his friend's fur.

"I am sorry, Cerberus. I know you didn't ask for any of this. No one did. It was a selfish anger driven plan." He shuddered. He had wiped out an entire pantheon. Lives upon lives. Temples had been smashed. Libraries burned down. Memories and stories wiped out. He had torn everything apart because he was tired of living in the shadows. Hades had become tired of not having his wife with him when she wanted to be. She was his sunlight and he had been tired of the cold. He was tired of the screams from Tartarus. The last straw of everything when he had heard the cries of his wife and son when Hera had the child murdered out of jealousy. Then Zeus had finally claimed the child he sired. Supposedly to keep the Underworld from influencing the child too much and to save that which belonged to the reigning god.

It had been what had driven Persephone to agree to his plan. A child she had been raising and loved was torn from her when it suited Zeus. He had not helped until the Titans had only left the heart of the child for last. No one else had been asked if they wanted to be removed from existence and memory. It had just been Persephone he had asked. It had been the two of them that erased *their* child. Erased Cerberus. Erased Demeter, Artemis, Charon, and everyone else from the pantheon.

He didn't even understand how Stephen had retained his memories. Was that why his brother had always been angry at him? Did his brother always know who he was? What about Idris? Oh gods, he needed to call him too. Would Idris hate him? Poseidon tended to be stormy on a good day. A bad day had a tendency to be catastrophic. Was Idris even really Poseidon?

Tahvo's heart hurt. His head hurt. His body felt like crap and that the careful control he tried hard to maintain had crumbled. It was hard to feel like he made any good choices. Lyric was heartbroken over her mother. He lost his temper *again*. It was something he was not remotely proud of and he wasn't even sure where to start handling that. It could continue to harm his... well Lyric wasn't technically his wife now, was she? No doubt she could now have the freedom to choose another. Something he feared and yet... he just hoped for something better for her sake. No matter how deeply he loved her, he couldn't be so selfish.

In this life, Tahvo was not known as a cold frightening force that made people tremble when they heard his name. Tahvo Melanthios was the veterinarian that worked late nights into early mornings making sure surgeries went well. That animals had the best comforts while they recovered. That the lost could find a home. The sick could pass in peace. All of these things dealt with those living. Trying to keep animals alive for their sake and the sake of the people that the animals claimed as theirs. To ease those into gentle slumber when life gave pain that was too much for them.

"Thank you for raising me again, Tahvo." The sudden voice was a soft throaty whisper. The sound of it broke Tahvo out of his train of thought as he lifted his head from dark fur. Spot's head was craned back and as soon as their eyes met, he licked Tahvo's cheek.

When his human just stared at him in utter confusion, Spot tried again, "You can understand me, right? Or is your head still bog-"

"You're talking to me! I can- I can understand you!" He stared at his Cerberus who seemed amused as he cocked his head and pressed his cold nose on Tahvo's cheek and sprawled over his lap.

"Don't need to yell. I am right here. Old dog ears still work well." Then Spot added pitifully, "Although if you are reaaaaaallly sorry, I will accept being allowed to eat a burger on the bed."

"You are allowed to eat in the bedroom, but I am *not* letting you eat in the bed. Especially not a burger. You will drool on everything and I didn't buy a water bed." Tahvo rubbed at his eyes before he gave a scratch around the collar on the neck. He was talking to Cerberus! He was *understanding* him!

"Damn. Well, at least I am still getting a burger. Can I eat with Asteri? I like her. I am glad she isn't one of us." Spot said as he closed his eyes and let out a dog huff of air as he relaxed with the attentive hands scratching all of those spots he just couldn't get himself. Honestly, Hades had always been his favorite person. Persephone was his second favorite of course.

"I am glad too. Not sure if she could have survived the memory flood." Tahvo admitted quietly. A frown formed, "I wonder how many of us remembered. Gods, I really hope no one was doing anything dangerous or driving when that happened. Once they figure out who I am, I am probably in for a rude awakening. Do you know what is going to happen once everyone figures out they were gods or other beings of myth and legends? Ones with *magic*? Mortals with god-like magic on Earth. Sounds like a nightmare."

"Guess that part wasn't exactly thought through very well. I'd help, but I am a tenth of what I used to be."

"Well, I wouldn't change a thing about you except to make you not hurt, buddy." Tahvo assured his friend. A hug of the dog and he kissed the top of his head affectionately. While he never had a child of his own, having raised the hound from infancy in both life-times made the dog nearly like a child to him. Probably another reason he spoiled the hell out of him.

In all honesty, Tahvo probably would be the first person to admit that Cerberus was his furry four-legged child. If he got sick, Tahvo was nearly just as sick from worry. When Cerberus had reached milestones of growth and learned new tricks, Tahvo was deliriously proud. When the dog had gone through the training needed as a puppy into adulthood to be a service animal for him, the hound took to it like a fish in water. There was very little Tahvo did not love about the dog other than the fact his friend couldn't live as long as a human did. Although with Pandora's box open and magic being relearned, one had to wonder about immortality. Did they still need the ambrosia and nectar?

Spot let out a long yawn and nuzzled his head against Tahvo's stomach, "I'll be fine. Just need lots of food, sleep, and pets. You are always good at those. Though you better mate with Lyric soon before you two are in a park and a little kid is asking why you two are wrestling behind a tree."

"Cerberus!"

"What? Do you know how many animals I see at the park doing the dirty outside in the daylight? I mean come on, there are children around. Children don't understand what those ducks are doing. Though it is really funny watching the parents get all-"

"Cerberus, really, just stop." Tahvo groaned, rubbing his head. Then he felt his heart drop into his stomach as he heard giggling from the doorway. A single glance and he could see Lyric failing to hide her laughter as she held a plate of several burgers in one hand. Her other hand car-ried a plate of cooked beef patties. Suddenly, Spot found the energy to hop off of the bed and slowly trot over and snuffled at the air.

"Ooh, I knew I liked you for a reason." Spot said happily as he looked past her to the little black and white dog behind her legs, "Hey Asteri. How about we go eat and check on the puppies. There is a giant pet bed in there that feels like a cloud. I'll show you it."

Lyric just laughed more and handed Tahvo the plate of burgers, "Eat something while I go feed these two. Then I can see how I feel about some of that mating Spot was talking about."

Seeing Tahvo's face go absolutely red was entirely worth it. Especially as he saw Cecilia and Orion in the hall with James and Marco staring in like a bunch of nosy children trying to spy. What in the name of Styx were they doing?

"Would you just all go eat or something? You all act like you have never seen someone flirt before." Tahvo huffed, face red as he shooed them all away. He was barely mollified when Lyric bent down to gift him a tiny kiss before skipping off with the plate of patties to give the pair of dogs. Tahvo was suddenly glad those two were fixed. No puppies were in his future. No matter how friggin cute they might be, he didn't need to add to the puppy population he already took care of.

Besides, having Spot teach the lot how to harass him was probably not the greatest idea.

While Lyric was gone, James grinned devilishly as he poked his head into the room, "We just haven't ever seen *you* flirt, Boss. Anyway, we are gonna eat then check the clinic and then head out. Tell Lyric thank you for dinner. If you need anything, remember to call. In case of a fire always stop, drop, and roll and remember-"

"Wrap it before you tap it!" Cecilia shouted gleefully before spinning with a laugh and hauling her husband down the hall and making the others follow as Tahvo glared after them. Anything he wanted to yell after them came out in an incoherent sputter as he heard the faint beautiful laughter of Lyric down the hall.

Still... he couldn't help but smile in exasperation. Even if he was horrendously embarrassed by it all, his friends were a rather amusing bunch. To be honest, he was glad he had them. Seeing Cecilia with Orion was one of the good things he had done. Honestly, he was hoping there was more good than bad results after this latest bout of magic. Logically he knew it was too late now to beat himself up over it. All he could do now was figure out how to make the most of the second chance to the best of his abilities. Not to mention survive the wrath of those who undoubtedly felt wronged by him.

Perhaps that included what Spot had so delicately called 'mating'. After all, no other person had ever gotten his heart to race as soon as he saw their smile. The way his breathing caught when she walked back into the room with nearly glowing eyes and flushed cheeks that might have been red from embarrassment or laughter. He was willing to bet it was a mixture of both.

Lyric smiled as she gently closed the bedroom door and sat on the bed next to Tahvo with a companionable silence. Stealing a burger, she devoured the thing like it was the last food on Earth. Having something that didn't come from a fast food restaurant was such a miracle. Somehow such a small thing nearly made Lyric feel spoiled and over indulgent.

The fact that food felt over indulgent would probably be something to infuriate poor Tahvo more than he was with the way she had been living up until that point. So she decided to make the diplomatic decision not to mention that little detail at all. No reason to upset and stress him more than he already had been. Instead she decided to lean her body against his as she ate. Eyes closing as she took in the almost quiet. The sounds of James' car starting and driving away was soft. No doubt the Bowet's vehicle was at the clinic.

"I missed Cecilia. Her and I used to play and hunt all of the time when I had been Kore." Lyric admitted softly. A fond smile as she added, "I am so glad she found Orion again. When Apollo had done what he did to her out of jealousy, I had been so angry on her behalf. Charon and the Minotaur was kind of a surprise. They are cute together though. They get all huffy about who gets things on the high shelves. James wants to do it all on his own."

Tahvo listened to her. A proper smile was showing as she kept babbling about the things she learned. People she was curious to see. What people she looked forward to seeing and which ones she could do without meeting. The way she pondered what tragedies they possibly mended with this new start was another subject she brought up. Lyric seemed so hopeful and focused on what good this new life could have given them all.

It was an endearing trait that had made her the sunlight in his dark world. An incredibly happy voice that he could listen to for hours on end. If he were trying to sleep, her melodic voice could soothe any nightmare.

The meal passed quickly after both realized just how hungry they were. Soon they were both just laying in the bed, still in their clothes from earlier. Lyric had tucked herself against the side of his body, absently chattering away about whatever her mind was thinking about. It had gone from the new starts to things about what she used to do when she had been a god. People she played with and befriended. Stories he heard a thousand times in their past, but he certainly couldn't complain about hearing them now. When she started on the things she missed about him though, he was utterly stunned.

Occasionally, Tahvo would answer her questions with his thoughts when she asked who else he met was a god and which god or person of legend they may have already met. While Tahvo did not say too much, he was happy to let her talk. It was not something he generally did much himself in fear of saying something inane.

"You are being awfully quiet. You are sure I am not boring you?" Lyric asked for the third time. She seemed to pout when he started laughing at her and the complete innocence in her voice. If only she could understand how much he truly did not mind if she talked until the sun set and rose again a thousand times over.

"My sun and song, I promise you I am simply delighting in the sound of your voice." He kissed the top of her head, "I am getting the opportunity to learn so much about this new you."

Lyric continued to pout at him, "You aren't patronizing me, right? How in the world are you not bored?"

"Ah, because you are enchanting, Lyric. If I was cursed to forget you every day for the rest of my soul's existence, I could rest easy knowing the delight I feel learning about you now will continue day after day."

"Well, I hope you don't forget me." Lyric said softly. His words made her want to nearly cry from the overwhelming emotion washing over her, "There is more than a day's worth to know about me."

"We have a lifetime to relearn each other. I shall never ever be bored." Tahvo grinned at her with utter adoration in his eyes. He could not help himself around her when she was so at ease.

Gods, despite the previous circumstances of how she met Hades, she was so very happy she had met him at all. If they had any Fates in existence in this new life, they were certainly smiling upon them now. She silently thanked them for giving her the chance to meet him again.

Lyric moved to place her hand on his chest. She could feel his heart racing faster through his shirt from just her touch. Idly, she started to drag her short nails against the buttons on his shirt. There was a need to feel his skin with her own. A need to be as close to him as physically possible.

"Tahvo, I really want to kiss you again." Honestly, Lyric wanted to do so very much more than that, "May I kiss you?"

That she still felt the need in her to ask him permission was deeply touching. Such dedication to forming a new habit made him want to do the same for her. It was certainly an arousing form of foreplay to hear what she wanted to do.

"I would love if you kissed me. Though I would love to do far more with you." He admitted in a voice that dropped slightly in the sudden realization of need.

A shiver of anticipation ran through her at the very thought of more. Not having a nurse to interrupt them, or Fates knew what, would be incredibly promising. Her imagination started to wander as she imagined the ways he *used* to do things with her. Memories of the kisses along her body and hands skimming over her skin caused her to get goosebumps.

As a gentle encouragement, she started to run her hand in slow circles over his racing heart, "Tell me what kinds of things you would like to do to me, Tahvo. I want to hear it." Her voice a tremor, "I want to imagine it by just the sound of your voice."

How did he begin to respond to that? There was so much he wanted to do with her. Did he go over every step? Teasingly gloss over all of the most intimate moments? Tahvo wanted her to understand just how attentive to her body he wished to be. His gaze rove over the length of her body. He was considering where he wanted to start. With his eyes ensnaring hers, he started to trace his finger tips from behind her ear to her collar bone.

"I would like to shower you with the softest kisses from your neck and work my way down. After that, I want to kiss your hips and work my way up as I peel back your shirt." Tahvo told her with a thick voice as need swelled up inside of him.

The air rushed out of her lungs from the very thought. Her imagination ran wild. Merciful gods, she hoped no one else interrupted them for a good long while. He was off to a good start and she wanted to feel his lips on her skin with such a burning need.

"What else?"

"Well hmm... I want to hear your sounds as I scrape my teeth lightly across your breasts." He continued, voice deepening as it fell to a whisper. Tahvo's hand slid along the length of her arm and took the hand tracing circles on his chest, "I would very much like to continue describing all of these things to you as your hand cups my erection. I want you to feel how much I want to do these things to you. Lyric, may I please move your hand?"

He was asking her. Lyric felt herself giving a tremulous smile, "Yes, please. I want to feel you too. I want my skin touching yours so very badly. I want to hear your every sound as you imagine what my body will feel like tangled with yours."

Muscles tightened down low on Tahvo's body in a very sudden and desperate need to feel her warmth surround him in every sense of the word. Very slowly he guided her hand over his belly and down to the button of his pants. While she threaded the button through the loop, his nails skimmed over her wrist. Goosebumps pebbled all along her arm as he felt her shiver.

Lyric quickly had his pants undone, zipper and all. She felt him guide her hand again and first push it down over the cloth covering it. It was warm there and she could feel the dampness starting to soak through as her fingers ran over him. Then there was a realization that the length of her hand could never entirely cup all of him. His breath caught as he let her explore him with her hand over him. His fingers merely laid twitching on the back of her hand as she started to slowly stroke the underside through the fabric. His breathing started to form into short pants as he tried to hold back sounds of pleasure.

When she finally slid her hand up to the waist band and down past to feel that velvet-soft skin, he gasped and groaned. Lyric could feel as he stilled himself while his mind came undone at just that simple touch. Her hand remained still where it was, cupping him as he had asked her to do in the first place. His tip was tucked against her palm as she watched him try and center himself.

"Are you alright?" Lyric asked softly, watching his eyes half-close and in a haze.

A nod after a few deep breaths. Tahvo hadn't expected it to feel that good. It had taken so much of him to not roll her under him and pin her. He realized he had been so very glad he asked her. Most people didn't particularly care about consent. They often used body language, but that was also how people became confused and misinterpreted signals. A mistake he didn't want to make with her.

He was bound and determined to do this right. Perhaps that was why they kept getting so close and then something came up. Something was always stopping them from going any further than a kiss. Yet, Tahvo wanted her to choose this with him, and he was going to give it to her. Impulses be damned.

"I have discovered that speaking is going to be.... slightly difficult." He admitted. A thin smile showing as he resisted the urge to grind against her hand. Another few deep breaths as he looked at her with drowning eyes. The look of someone who wanted the other in the most carnal way possible.

Somehow, he was going to make this work.

"I want to take all of your clothing off of you without hesitation, Lyric." He admitted, "Every part of me wants to feel your skin against mine as I let you undress me and take your every pleasure from me. I want to feel your mouth on my need as you torment me to the very edge. I want to roll you under me and taste every inch of you with my tongue as you writhe and moan."

Tahvo forced himself still he spoke, voice a trembling whisper as he held her gaze with his. His imagination was the very worst kind of torture. He had clearly been doing his job wrong when he had those cruel souls in Tartarus. Torment was nowhere near as painful as pleasure withheld.

Patience was not exactly Lyric's strong suit. Instead she moved to straddle his hip while she laid along his side, her hand gently stroking his length, "You have but to ask me, Tahvo."

He managed to shake his head slightly, "No, I want to do this right. I want you to *know*." Tahvo needed her to ask.

Needed her to want this as much as he did. Any steps taken, he wanted her consent without feeling like she only did it because he wanted to. Hells thrice damn those that made it seem as though women were merely there for the beck and call of men.

Ever since he had met her, he had wanted to give her everything she could have ever asked for. If she would have asked for him to jump, he would ask how high. Except she had not ever taken advantage of him in such a way. Nothing selfish was ever asked for. Only had ever asked for love and his time.

"Then tell me, Tahvo. Please let me know how much you want this." Lyric whispered close to his ear before kissing his jaw. Nuzzling his skin.

A swallowed lump in his throat as he tried to figure out how to breath. Her hand was so warm. Her leg had hooked around his and that thigh just barely brushed against the base of his erection where her hand did not cover, "I want to fill you to brimming. I want to give you everything I never could as the God of the Underworld." He was already bad at words before, this made him afraid to screw up as he tried to find the words needed to explain the roaring emotions inside of him.

Tentatively, he opened his eyes and chanced a look at her. Those golden eyes met his green ones and he saw the tinge of confusion in her eyes. Lyric did not know what in the world he could give her now that he had not before. Of course, part of him was afraid to say that one thing.

Children were not always the next step after a relationship. Perhaps it had in the past, but Persephone had wanted children. Lyric could have very well decided not to want any in this life. That was something that either felt like freedom or entrapment. Despite the fact they were going through with this, there was no way Tahvo was going to assume she was going to stay with him and only him.

Sparks didn't always take to kindling to start a fire. The god knew all too easily that a spark could have very easily sat and smoldered until its glow faded. He hated being dishonest. Hated even more to hide something as important as that.

"I want to give you choice. I want you to have the freedom of the choice to be with me. To ensure you can always walk in the sunlight and freedom to come and go whenever you want." He told her softly. Then he looked down at himself and then considered his next question before realizing a huge mistake he made in all of this, "I don't have condoms."

Lyric blinked at him, sitting up a bit. Now she was really confused, "What?"

"Condoms. I don't have any."

"What do..."

"Lyric, we have only met a few days ago. Literally. I know we have *known* each other in a past life, but that was a different-" He made a strangled sound and thumped his head back into the pillows hard, "We are us. Persephone wanted children. Hades was not an anxiety-ridden mess. You may not necessarily want children or... or want me."

The way he said that last part was so heartbreaking. Lyric watched him look at her with pleading eyes. He was trying so hard. For his sake, she drew her hand out of his pants and cupped his face gently. That tormented look appeared at the very action and she wished she could find a way to help. It hurt to know that he was right. What if they *didn't* want each other in the end? Hell, Lyric still had no idea if she ever wanted children or not. What if she became like her mother?

"We don't have to have *sex*, Tahvo. Not the traditional way at least." Her voice was soft as she tried to soothe his fears, "I honestly don't know if I want children or not. The idea terrifies me. Having memories of the last time does not help any... I couldn't protect him."

He nodded numbly at her, "I never want to do that to you. I don't ever want you to feel trapped because of me." Eyes closed as he turned his face to nuzzle her hand. A small comfort as he tried to desperately ignore the aching between his legs. It was a painful reminder at just how bad he was at this. How bad he was at people in general. How could he possibly function in a long term relationship. Gods help him, he didn't want to become her regret.

Lyric hugged him, moving her leg away from his need so that she didn't torture him more than he was. What did she even say to that? Suddenly all of her words dried up and she just hugged him tight. Most of the pills and anything that involved hormones being introduced into her body had always made her sick. Condoms had always been her go to solution. Except she had never thought to ever get any. Never thought she was ever going to have sex any time soon, especially not after what Stephan did. After that, the idea of a relationship had scared her.

"Would it be... easier if we waited?" Lyric asked.

"No." He answered truthfully, "I don't think so. I mean... I don't know what would be easier. I want to... I want to do so much with you. I also don't want to screw up my second chance with you. The right thing is never easy."

Tahvo grimaced and sat up. He moved to slightly side back and prop his back against the headboard of his bed, "If I am not careful to decide my every action, I become impulsive. I make rash decisions and... I don't want to do that with you. I know policing my every action just creates more anxiety but I have seen what happens when I don't take the care needed to keep from making mistakes that could harm others."

Lyric sat up with him. Her arms wrapped carefully around his waist. Those moments he had been impulsive, she had seen the good and bad of it. The things that could happen could have effects that might complicate things more than needed. Burrowing against him, she tried to figure out what to say that might help.

"You feel best when I *choose* and guide what happens, right?" Lyric watched him nod slightly, "But you aren't comfortable with just pleasure for yourself because you are worried about losing control."

"Right." He said softly. Tahvo sighed, "And I am... not sure how I feel about getting pleasure if I cannot give it in return. I hate... I overthink it all. I can't focus on my pleasure if I am too worried about if you are getting any."

"In a way, it is incredibly sweet that you are so very concerned about my well-being. It is going to end up killing you though if you keep it up." Lyric told him softly. Then she gave a little bit of a lopsided smile, "Just how 'innocent' are you?"

"Innocent?"

"Like, if you did have sex, how ah... creative are you?"

"I would like to think I was as creative as one could get without needing a... ah safe word." Tahvo frowned at her for a long moment, "It is not like I have had sex often. It is a sparing thing I did with very few people. Usually after I knew them for a while."

"Ah, so you are more demi." Lyric said thoughtfully before she smiled at his confusion. Had to wonder just how *creative* he did get in this life-time. Though she was willing to bet he didn't take consent to such scrutiny that they were right then. When it came to her, it seemed like his mind went into an utter panic. He wasn't sure what to do with himself. The situation between them was as fragile as the thinnest coat of ice over a lake in the winter.

"Demi?"

"Demi-sexual. You don't form a sexual attraction unless you form a close bond. I am throwing everything off kilter because part of you... part of *us* had a close bond already. Tahvo doesn't have a close bond with Lyric. Hades *does* however, have a close bond with Persephone."

Well, that made sense. It was accurate, "Explains quite a bit. It sort of feels like there are suddenly two people in the same body. Two births. Two sets of memories and experiences." He seemed to relax a little when they were focusing on something more... analytical. So far, he hadn't gotten to form a close bond at all with Lyric yet. Not as he generally did with anyone, "But I *am* sexually attracted to you. I just feel... horribly conflicted about it."

"Probably makes your brain question the legitimacy of how you feel." Lyric nuzzled his chest slightly, "But, we can solve the need for pleasure without anyone aching for release and making decisions that could lead to other panic inducing situations. I heard '69 was a good year after all."

"Good year, what the..." Tahvo stared at her before it clicked and he blinked, cheeks burned then, "Oh. Did you... did you just make a joke about oral sex?"

"I could start making jokes about what to call your erection. I have a ton of them now. Very punny things. Remember stamen? I mean I can make rigor mortis jokes now. Or even baby gravy cannon. Purple hel-"

"Please, no. No baby gravy cannons for my penis, thank you." Tahvo screwed up his face. Seriously, saying that out loud in any romantic context just seemed.... silly. Of course he very clearly remembered the stamen incident. Her demands, loud demands, for a deflowering with his 'stamen' once several hundred years into their marriage had been hilarious. In that very cringe worthy sort of way that made him glad at times that they didn't have many people that heard her demands.

"But don't all guys call their penises something clever?"

"I am certain only by those who brag. I don't know. Stephen probably called his a thunderbolt when we were growing up." Tahvo never saw a reason to actually call it anything crude or corny.

"What? Flashy and impressive at a distance, but you wouldn't want it anywhere near you?" Lyric snorted a bit and then shook her head. They were getting off topic. A shift to move to her knees and look him in the eyes, "But, we aren't talking about him. He doesn't matter. *You* matter.

Not Hades, but Tahvo." Her voice was soft as she focused on the man before her.

Her words brought his attention to the present and not their past. For now, they could focus on what they needed presently. Which for them both seemed to be a release. Mutual pleasure that could be done without having to worry about children following.

"Next shopping trip, we are buying condoms." He told her as he looked down into her eyes, "Lyric Helios, may I please kiss you? May I please give you pleasure?"

Oh yes, they were definitely doing that. Lyric then studied him before she whispered her answer with as much sincerity as possible. Couldn't let him doubt her want in this, "Yes for all of it, Tahvo. Please. *Yes*."

Tahvo laced his fingers into her hair and drew her up to him, "As you wish." Then he pressed his lips against hers.

9

With complete permission given, Tahvo was able to focus on deep and thorough kisses. His hands slid down to her hips so that he could pull at the hem of her shirt. As soon as he drew back for air, that shirt was tugged up and over her head. The two weren't wasting time in being methodical this time. Neither wanted the other to overthink themselves into a corner again. Nor did they want interrupted.

They were going to do this. They were going to lose themselves in the pleasure they allowed. Which meant that question of pleasure covered all the bases. Although he kept a mindful eye and ear for if she did not enjoy something.

Those gloriously golden browns travelled down his body. Lyric drank in his appearance as she unbuttoned his shirt right after he pulled hers off. Before he could draw her in for another kiss, her head dipped down to do something she had wanted to do since she saw him shirtless the first time. Her lips pressed against his collar bone and then she nipped hard at the skin, almost hard enough to draw blood.

That sudden sharp pain made Tahvo moan. His hands moved to steady himself on the bed as his head swam. It stung so sweet when mingled with the drunken pleasure of kissing her. She followed that bite with a gentle lick that made his arms want to go limp. Then she continued her pleasant madness with little licks, kisses, and gentler nibbles down the line of his body.

Finally, he was able to move one hand to sink into her bright hair. Fingers tangled into the curls and nails scraped against her scalp as he kneaded it. Her answering moan let him know he was doing something she liked. An encouragement to continue even as she got lower and lower to the most aching part of him.

When Lyric reached his hip, he fought not to just flip her over and pin her under him. Instead he obligingly lifted his hips up for her as she slid down his pants and boxers together. Kisses rained on his hips and thighs. Her lips never actually touched anywhere near his erection, but her hair flowing over it had him nearly panting again from overwhelming need.

"I thought I was supposed to be pleasing *you* with showers of kisses all over your body." He complained weakly.

"Well, maybe having you at my whims is just as pleasurable to me." Lyric responded with a little smirk.

"So long as I... as I get..." Tahvo's words vanished at the long lick on the underside. He nearly whimpered in pure frustration, "I am trying to speak."

Lyric gave him only a slightly sympathetic smile, "Is it bad to not feel sorry for being so good at being distracting?"

Head shook at her as he kneaded her scalp with a flex of his hand, "Just make sure I get a turn to taste you too."

"I will, my Tahvo." Her voice was soft and she moved to run her hands over his swollen length, "Just let me appreciate every inch of you. After all, I am a very dominant person in bed and I can't help but to enjoy having you at my every whim."

"Oh really? Would have never-" He groaned as she licked him again, effectively ending the thick sarcasm. Was she *trying* to egg him on? A mock glare at her as she smiled oh so impishly back at him.

"Something the matter, Tahvo? You seem to have a problem with that whole speaking thing. Course maybe you are just being a very good listener."

A huff at her and he tugged gently on her hair in warning, "Keep that up, Lyric, and I'll show you that I can be dominant too."

Eyes glittered at his promising threat, wanting so very badly to test his word. A smile shone as she leaned down and flicked the tip of her tongue to catch the seeping cum off of his tip. There was a small unhindered thrust into the air. She stole that opportunity to open her mouth wide and slide him into her warm mouth.

Tahvo let out a strangled cry as he forced himself still and managed not to orgasm from just that. He fisted his hand in her hair and chanced a look down at her. When their eyes met, he felt like he somehow hardened more at the incredibly erotic sight. It seemed as though she had been waiting for him to be watching her. With her mouth full, she slowly started to take more of him in.

The tip was felt being pushed down her throat. It felt so incredible and it nearly made Tahvo delirious in pleasure. Worry won out and though he wished he could just lay there and enjoy the act, he couldn't do that without making sure she wasn't hurting herself.

He untangled his hand from her hair and moved to grasp at one of her hands. His fingers curled around hers to make sure she could have a secure grip, "Lyric, are you alright? One squeeze for yes. Two if you are hurting, alright?" The words were soft and trembling as it was hard to form anything coherent. She responded with one short squeeze and she continued until he was hilted entirely in her mouth and throat.

Lyric couldn't breathe properly like this, but she managed to slowly bob her head up and down a few inches for a couple of movements. Entirely worth it to hear his moan cutting through the sound of blood rushing through her ears. Her lungs burned for air though and she needed to breathe again. So she very carefully drew back and let go of him with a soft popping sound. Lyric sat back on her heels as she worked on reacquainting herself with air.

"I hurt you, didn't I?" Tahvo asked softly. Being large was not necessarily always a good thing. Her face was flushed and eyes watery from that little act. No matter how good it felt, he didn't want her hurt because of it. He held her hand securely, waiting for her to answer him before he did anything else.

"I'm fine, Tahvo." She breathed, words all too soft. A cough and a clearing of her throat and she was better, "I chose to do that. I wanted you to at least be able to hilt yourself in me at least once. Besides, I always wanted to do that to someone uncircumcised." She then leaned forward and kissed him softly to reassure him. Her words at least offered a little comfort.

"Well, when we are engaged in mutual pleasure, I want you to be able to breathe." He kissed her in return. Then he suddenly wrapped an arm around her waist and dragged her onto his lap. While she still had her jeans on, its rough texture didn't stop him from grinding his length against her.

"My turn to taste you, my impish jewel." He gave her a low and possessive growl.

Even with her jeans on, she could feel his warmth and hardness rubbing against her. A shudder in pleasure as she rocked against him. His words drove a hot spike of need right through her and she watched him with intense curiosity.

Tahvo smiled at her as he looked her over while she was perched on his lap. She was absolutely breathtaking. Those flushed cheeks and pleasure-dazed eyes coupled with those heavy breaths made him feel so very wanted. No matter what happened later, he knew that right at the moment her undivided attention was on him. He planned to make sure she got the same in return.

Lifting her up, he used his teeth to pull at the cup of her bra down enough to nuzzle against the swell of her breast. Enough of a yank down to spill enough out to trap it outside of the cup and he kissed the skin right beside the nipple. That soft sensitive skin tasted so very wonderful as he took some of that skin between his teeth and started to suckle hard.

Lyric threw her head back as she moaned. It was a wonderful distraction for him to unclasp her bra blindly, allowing it to fall loose enough that he was able to slip his hand under the band of it. His fingers gently rolled her nipple between them, causing her to gasp at that unexpected jolt of pleasure.

Hips danced and ground against him as small sounds escaped her throat. Lyric felt as though her head was spinning when he finally drew back with scraping teeth. He gave the new dark spot a soft kiss and drew back enough for her to see the red-violet mark that shone starkly against her skin. All of those thoughts scattered when he took as much of her breast into his mouth as possible and swirled his tongue against her hard nipple. She cried out softly at the sensation making her blind to him sliding the bra off of her arms.

He drew back with a small nip on her soft skin before doing the same to her other breast. He made slow circles with his thumb over the swollen breast before drawing back and looking up at her. Her breathing was quick and shallow and he could feel her heart racing so close to his fingers.

"Does that feel good?" Tahvo's voice was deep and husky as he watched her tremble. No doubt that part of her rubbing against him was aching. She nodded with short little bobs and he laughed, hot breath spilling over flesh as he kissed over her heart, "What's that? I can't hear your head rattle, my jewel."

"Tahvo, plea-" She yelped at the lightest nip on her nipple. A faux pout given to him, "That wa-" Another little yelp of surprise, but this time because he suddenly rolled her onto her back. His mouth roughly claimed hers while his hands busied themselves with her pants.

The scrape of his nails over sensitive skin was as intoxicating as his hungry kiss. An actual whine crawled out of her throat when he slowly drew back enough so their eyes could meet. Lyric could see how need and want warred in his eyes. He wanted to be inside of her desperately. He needed to do this right, and she knew that. Both of them wished so hard that he could bury himself deep inside of her,

Instead, his need won out and he reluctantly drew back after a short kiss on the lips. Then soft kisses fluttered over her ribs as he made a path down her body. Hands held her hips elevated so that when he got down, he could just kiss at the edge where soft curls of black hair teased his cheeks.

He nibbled over the ridge of her hip bone, making her dance under him. A small pleading sound escaped with her so very close to him. Lyric wanted him to taste her. Wanted him to stop tormenting her so well. Patience was not a virtue she had.

"Ask me, Lyric. I am yours to command." Tahvo whispered to her, "Ask me to please you. To drive you mad with need until you are begging for release."

"Please, Tahvo. Will you please... please do whatever you want." Lyric begged softly. Right now, she just wanted to feel him take his time with making her cry out in ecstasy. Thinking was the very last thing she wanted to be doing right then.

"Well, my jewel, I need *you* to tell me what to do. How else will I know the best ways to make you cry out for me?" He smirked at her deviously. Her exasperation was adorable. As encouragement, he moved down and flicked the tip of his tongue against the cluster of nerves that made the sensitive nub on her clit.

Lyric gasped and her hands clutched at the covers, "Oh gods, Tahvo, *please* keep doing that. Use your mouth on me and put that tongue to use. I want to feel your hand too. I want to feel you inside of me so badly."

"As you wish." He acquiesced by giving a good long lick from the bottom of her folds right up to the top. His long hair enshrouded his face, making the dark waves of his hair tickle the inside of her thighs. It made her hips jump and he laughed at her ticklishness.

While he would have loved to have teased her more, she had asked of him the pleasure of his mouth. Tahvo shifted to spread her legs out wide and parted her folds with his fingers so he could taste them. Incoherent sounds started filling his ears as she jerked and danced with his mouth. A nibble here and there, long licks along the sides with a careful avoidance at the most sensitive spot.

Then he slid two fingers into her, feeling that slick warmth and wishing it was a different part of his body buried within her. He started massaging inside of her, working to find that little spot that was oh so sensitive and- he heard her cry out his name. A small smile against her as he buried his mouth against her with a focus on suckling right on that little nub.

White light exploded behind her eyes and Lyric's body arched as she came hard and fast. He didn't stop either, no, he kept working his fingers inside of her. She could feel the scrape of his teeth against sensitive skin and his tongue dipping into her to drink down her pleasure. He rolled one orgasm into another one and she cried out and buried her fingers into his hair. Good gods, she didn't want him to stop, but she also wanted to get him to come too.

"T-Tahvo. S-stop." She pleaded regretfully. To her surprise, he stopped on the dime and stared up at her. Confusion in his eyes as she looked at him dazed. "We were going to... the thing. Words not working."

Oh. Yes, she had wanted to make sure they *both* got release. Tahvo backed off, though he almost gave her after another lick. Lyric watched as he drew his fingers from her and promptly licked them. Her mouth went dry and she make a strangled sound before she sat up. Oh she was so going to feel more of that glorious mouth and she was determined for him to find pleasure from hers.

"Tomorrow. Store. Condoms." Lyric told him before pushing him back onto the bed. His soft 'oomph' made her feel victorious as she crawled up him and kissed him, tasting herself on his lips.

Tahvo made a sound of assent. He watched her draw back from him and maneuver herself with a little uncertainty to where she faced away from him. She was straddled over his face, her knees on either side of his head. He smoothed his palm over her ass and then ran his nails over it. He couldn't see what she was doing this way, but he sure as hell felt it as he felt her start licking his tip.

Determined to return the favor, he groaned and spread her apart enough to drop her hips down low to him and he began to lick her thoroughly. Her sensitivity to having already orgasmed worked well in his favor as she made little sounds as she tried to focus on coating every inch of him with her tongue. He rubbed his thumb against that sensitive nub while he devoured her as though trying to clean her. It was an exercise in pleasant futility as she was crying out again.

That methodical rhythm of his thumb and mouth soon became erratic as she took as much of him into her mouth as she could without hindering her breathing. Her sounds vibrated through him as she bobbed her head up and down. Hair brushed against his balls and thighs as she covered the length of him not in her mouth with her slick hand. She came again and again as he made sure not to let up. An intense focus on making sure he milked every last orgasm out of her that she could stand. He had meant to warn her that he was about to cum, but suddenly he spilled out as his world was rocked. A loud moan as his mouth automatically kept going. Both hands clutched her hips tight as he made sure she came until she begged for him to stop or couldn't give another drop.

Her sweet revenge was to milk him just as much until he had to draw his head back, "Lyric." He rasped, "St-stop.

Too much." He nuzzled against her leg as she giggled breathlessly. He shuddered at even the feeling of her breath on him as he very slowly started going soft.

"Then, you stop too. I might become all sorts of dehydrated if you keep doing that to me." A flop as she rolled off of him and she slowly wiggled herself like an odd fish until she was heads up and snuggling against his side. That little show made him start laughing. Gods, he enjoyed watching her move, even if it was graceless.

"Your mouth felt amazing." He told her. Seriously, he had driven him absolutely mad in the very best way., "And you taste just as much so."

"Mm, you too." Lyric purred, snuggling happily against him, "But seriously. Tomorrow. Condoms. I am going to make sure I get to rock your world again and see your face when I do it."

"I did well enough for a second round?" He asked softly, a smile playing on his lips. Right then, he was content, if not a slight bit chilly laying on top of the covers instead of under them. Though her warmth beside him definitely helped combat that.

"Mm, yes. Though I am willing for a second round to be in a nice hot shower before bed." Lyric looked up at him and grinned, "Well, so long as the second round is a lot of kissing. Pretty sure anything else right now might be too much."

"Come again?" Tahvo smiled as she stared at him.

"You made a pun!"

"Yes, I have been known to do that on occasion." Laughter escaped his lips as she sat up. Apparently this was not something she had expected from him at all. It made him grin at her lazily, "Now then, would you like to come clean and get into the shower?"

"That was another pun! Who are you and what have you done with my husband?" Lyric asked before realizing what she said. That smile on Tahvo's features vanished as he just looked unsure and afraid suddenly. Afraid of how she would feel about those last two words she had said. In reality, if she picked apart the sentence literally, it was a can of worms they still hadn't entirely addressed yet.

Lyric must have been silent too long, as Tahvo seemed to withdraw out of that ease and comfort. Pain haunted his eyes as he gently peeled her arm off of him.

"I'll let you take the shower in here. I can use hallway bathroom. We should clean up and get some sleep. I'll take the dishes down as well. Thank you for dinner, Lyric."

"You're welcome, Tahvo." Was all she could manage to say. Not an apology or anything else. Everything else that came to mind seemed too pathetic. She watched him pull his boxers on and leave the room with the collection of dishes. Her heart weighed heavily as she watched him leave with doubt and fear in him. Dammit.

10

Lyric had gotten clean quickly after he left. It had been heartbreaking to do so alone as she realized that at some point he must have set all of her shower things on the shelf in the bathroom. Everything of hers had a place in there as though it already belonged. It felt like she belonged at his side, not because of their past, but because she felt content and comfortable with him in their present.

Yet, she was worried that he could never feel entirely comfortable with her. He would be so worried about if she wanted to be there because of him or because of Hades. While she did not mind reassuring him, but it was hard to be a hundred percent sure when he put it in a way that made it hard to question his logic. How could she assure him of this if she didn't feel one hundred percent sure herself? Was there something wrong when she may have wanted to be there for both reasons?

Lyric frowned as she stared at the mirror. Her damp hair smelled better at least, but the ends were still scorched and gnarled. A sigh as she dug into her bag in the bathroom for a zippered case and opened it to reveal a pair of shears, a texturizer, and a razor. It had helped to have a friend who taught her enough of the basics to get by. Hopefully she didn't screw it up too badly.

She combed it back as smooth as possible and tied it at the base of her neck. Fingers stubbornly making sure to smooth her curls as best she can. Pulling the rest of the hair over her shoulder, she stared at the damp hair starting to curl up as it dried. Well, it was now or never right? Could always get it fixed, but those burnt parts were a pain. She looked in the mirror and slipped the shears onto her hand and took a deep breath.

Tahvo wondered if he had overreacted as he stood in his room with only a towel around his waist. A frown at the silence of the house and wondered if Lyric was still there or not. Part of him really wanted to talk to her about what was said, but the other part of him was afraid that he would just stand there silently gaping like a fish. That or that she would entirely reject him for saying something completely inane.

Hair dripped water on his shoulders, causing little trails of water to run down his chest and back. As he got his clothes together the phone rang. A frown as it went a couple more rings until the answering machine in the room picked up. The little message played first and then a loud beep. Silence followed for a few moments before someone started speaking.

"Tahvo... Hades... whoever you are. It is Idris... Poseidon." A sound of annoyance before cursing, "Gods, you and Persephone made a downright fucking mess of things. Look, Stephen called me trying to get me to agree to kill you. Figured you should know our brother actually has it out for you. Also your house was all over the news this morning due to a fire, so pick up the phon-"

"Idris, why are you calling me?" Tahvo asked, picking up the phone immediately. A frown as he leaned against the dresser as he simply peeled off his towel to try and catch the drops of water from his hair. Damn hair always took forever and a year to dry.

"Were you standing and staring at the answering machine again?"

"Just answer the damn question, Idris."

"You know damn well why I called you. I mean hell, not like I got a concussion while driving. Nor have you bothered to call *me* yet."

Tahvo sighed and pinched his fingers on the bridge of his nose. Idris was forever charming when angry, "I had a concussion of my own. Stephen set the damn thing off in front of my face. Sorry I haven't called you yet. Honestly,

I wasn't sure if you really were you. That would have been awkward as well. Are you okay?"

That seemed to calm his sibling down a little, "I am alive. Annoyed, but alive. How the hell did you survive Stephen anyway? Don't you live alone and have only one guy and Fido working for you?"

"His name is Spot and I have more than one employee, Idris." Tahvo told him dryly, "But I survived because James and Marco had seen the fire. Marco had a few centuries worth of anger to take out on him. Though I think you are going to need to watch your own neck."

"Gonna have to be more specific. Which one of the many dick swimmers is pissed off at our brother for spawning them?"

"Not someone *he* sired. Mind you he did get with his grandmother. It is the Minotaur. You know, the poor soul born as a result of you making his mother have a weird ass fetish."

"Fuck. Why the hell am I watching my own neck? It isn't my fault she... okay it is but..." Idris made an annoyed sound on the phone.

"See? So learn to duck... or run very fast. Now then, are you are calling because you are genuinely worried about me or because you want a piece of my hide, because if it is the latter, get in line." Tahvo had a slightly better relationship with his other brother. Barely. Idris at least had the decency to be worried about him when things crashed down around his ears a few times as they grew up. Idris had the decency to not mock the problems he had.

"Shut up. I like my neck unsnapped. As for my call: both frankly, but honestly you could have done worse. You could have married Hera."

Tahvo stilled at that and stared at the phone as if his brother could feel him staring, "Wait, is Emily *the* Hera? How the hell did you marry her and not Amphitrite?"

"Well, that is the pain in the ass part." Idris mumbled as he added, "I am parked in front of your house. I would rather talk about this over something mind obliterating. So can you answer the door before Spot burns a hole into my head with his eyes through the window?"

Curiosity made Tahvo nod slowly, "Yeah, let me get dressed. I'll be down in a second. Is Hera with you? I need to know before Seph gouges her eyes out."

"Just come downstairs, Tahvo." Idris told him sourly before hanging up. Tahvo frowned at the phone and hung it up himself. He shifted to stand before staring at the woman staring at him like a cat caught simply unawares.

Lyric stared less because of the phone call and more because she was getting a proper view of his body at a pleasant distance. He was relaxed, hair dripping wet, and the light in the room cast such interesting shadows. Which made her forget that she was holding her towel tightly against her fingers until she looked down and blinked.

"I need a bandage... or those little butterfly sutures. Maybe both. I don't know." She looked down at her hand and frowned. Peeling the towel back from it, she winced.

"How did you cut yourself in the shower?"

His brother was momentarily forgotten as he looked over her hand. A deep frown when he saw the red on her shoulder smeared across the skin and then he saw the uneven short jagged ends of her hair, "You cut your hair? Why? We could have... Someone else could have done this."

Lyric frowned at him, "Because it was getting annoying and it was burnt and well... I have the shears. Why not do it myself now and fix it later?"

"I don't know? Maybe because you had just been hurt and were in the hospital and now you just hurt yourself again?" Tahvo rubbed his temples a moment and abandoned the line of thought as he distanced himself and quickly got dressed in boxers and pants, "My brother Idris is waiting for me. I need to let him inside. Wash your hand and-" He paused and moved the towel to look over her hand, "Keep pressure. Bandages are in the white plastic box under the sink. Antiseptic wipe, gauze, medical tape. I'll be right back up to help."

Lyric just nodded numbly at him, a frown pulling at her lips as he looked her over. His brother's name still nagged at her like something familiar. Shaking her head, she watched as Tahvo seemed to have a wall up between them.

Was it because his brother was here? Or was he still upset at her slip of words? Deciding not to press the issue for now, she instead went back into the bathroom. She washed her hand again and got the case out from underneath to make at least a haphazard dressing until Tahvo could do a better one. She dressed the injury quickly and she pulled her damp hair into a messy bun on her head to hide the disaster she made of it.

Lyric decided that it wasn't the best idea to just hide away upstairs. She wasn't a coward, really. Though Tahvo had a point about Hera. She really hoped that she wasn't there.

She felt her hands tremble a little as she came down the stairs. A frown when she didn't find them in the living room right away and she continued cautiously until she reached the kitchen. A slow blink at the tall male talking to Tahvo. He looked as far away from being related as possible with copper-red hair cut back short on the sides and styled on the top with wispy messy curls. He had a snug black shirt on that paired with jeans just as tight. The white leather jacket that matched his belt and boots was folded and sitting on the counter-top. Their eyes were the same green though and that was what marked them as relatives.

Though it wasn't why she was staring. She was staring because she *knew* exactly who he was, "Drizzy!"

Idris blinked, jaw dropping open to stare at her as she ran at him and hugged him tightly. He stared down at her and then looked at Tahvo with shock. Which delighted his brother, overriding the sibling's confusion much to Idris' annoyance.

Though the other male in the room seemed to be pouting as he was sipped a class of ice water, "Aw, Lyric, you are ignoring your best friend?"

Lyric blinked and let go of Idris as quickly as she had hugged him. With a spin, she stared at the third male in the room. A big giant grin plastered on her face, "Caelan! I didn't know your boyfriend was Tahvo's brother!"

Tahvo blinked slowly as he took a closer look at the male standing in the room. He had natural strawberry blonde hair that was long and braided back against his head. Bright candy red streaks were placed in it for a play of color. Then he eyeballed his brother who at least had the decency to look embarrassed.

"Wait, aren't you *married*, Drizzy!?" Lyric spun and gave such a disappointed look to Idris and then over at Caelan, "You know better than to date a married man! What have I told you about that?"

"Ask first if the other person wants to share." Caelan said innocently, "Which you know, I *meant* to ask. Really. What can I say, I like not being the only person. Being focused on all on my lonesome is so... eh I don't care for it. I don't mind if Drizzy has another lady. Which by the way a space opened up an-"

"Caelan, please stop. Also would the two of you please stop calling me that god awful name? It is Idris, not Drizzy." He grumped quietly. The blushing man rubbed his neck as he looked at Tahvo, "Oh don't give me that look. Just because *you* were the only monogamous one doesn't absolve you of jack shit. Seriously, wiping out the *entire pantheon*? I just found out I married *Hera* for crying out loud. Like that is definitely a can of worms I never wanted to touch."

"Idris, we could draw our family tree with a spirograph. Our entire pantheon was a can of worms. At least we aren't playing dueling banjos on a lyre anymore." Tahvo told him dryly. Then a look over Caelan, "I swear I have met you before."

"We have met. I've had top surgery since then." Caelan shrugged and then smiled brightly. Seeming pleased when Tahvo just accepted it with a nod, "Among other things. Same name as before. Probably why you are confused. The hormones have kicked in finally. We really need to get you away from work a lot more often. It's been what, five years?"

Had it been that long? Had his brother been *dating* Caelan that long? How the hell did he miss that one? Tahvo rubbed the bridge of his nose. Dear gods, they were not that far away from being screwed up as they had been before. Less bestiality this time at least. He really didn't need to know if that was a thing or not, else he was going to have to start drowning people in the rivers of Hades.

"I must be in a coma. Stephan knocked my ass out and I am in a coma. I cannot be having this conversation right now." Tahvo grumbled. He so was not the quiet and careful person of before. Then again being around his brothers brought out that part of him that he generally never indulged in. Even though he seldom reached out to see what exactly they were up to. Often times they just barged in.

"Well, let's put it this way, at least Zeus didn't sire Persephone with Demeter this time." A pause and then Idris looked at Lyric, "You *are* an adult, right?"

"Ooooh, wait, Lyric is Sephy??" Caelan interrupted and studied Lyric with scrutiny. Apparently, he had entirely missed the memo. He grinned at the woman who clearly looked like she was drowning in confusion, "Sweetie, I'm Amphitrite!"

Lyric just blinked slowly at them all, "Ooh... well that makes sense actually. Also, that trash is *not* my father! Ew! I am actually older than he is! Thank the current gods for that." She then looked at Tahvo who just seemed like he wanted to beat his head off a brick wall. While she wanted to reach out and make him feel better with a touch, she felt like that would probably worsen his mood.

"So, before we get further into the wonderful world of who is who and the fact I somehow knew you two before I knew Tahvo, we probably want more alcohol for this conversation. As neither of us have slept since we got out of the hospital." Something they probably would have done after a shower if she hadn't gone and screwed that up.

"Gods yes. Give me wine. I need wine and I am going to drink it all until I can proceed to not think about the logistical nightmare that comes with the fact that Poseidon and Hera have *children* together." Tahvo scowled as he stalked over to his refrigerator. Then he frowned, "And where *are* said children?"

"Currently visiting our father. I figured it best for them not to worry about that right now. As far as I am aware, they are very mortal and very innocent." Idris said softly.

His tone changed as he looked to his brother. It was a pleading look for understanding, "Emily left me and the kids as soon as she remembered. Probably went looking for Stephen."

Idris scowled when he spoke and then sighed as Caelan hugged against his side. Caelan stretched up onto his toes and kissed him on the cheek. Seeming to chase away some of the pain in him.

"Any idea if our father is mortal or not?" Tahvo asked warily as he pulled several chilled bottles out. Different kinds, usually reserved for whatever best suited dinner. He blinked as Lyric had already went and grabbed some glasses from his cabinet. He wanted to kick himself as he looked to her wordlessly helping. Lyric hadn't really done anything wrong, yet he was being a pain in the ass. One who was presenting himself as a snarky whining jerk.

"As far as I am aware, he seems normal. Makes me wonder what Mom was." Idris said as he looked over the bottles, deciding which one he wanted to drink. The sudden quiet beside him made him stop and look up, "Oh shit, Tahvo I'm sorry. I didn-"

Tahvo held up his hand and shook his head, "If she was anything, we can't ask her now. Let's just ingest as much alcohol as possible we try to wade through the fact we have mortals who are suddenly remembering they are gods. Not to mention we are getting our magic back. Or the question of our current life spans or what happens now that we have our memories."

There was a hesitant nod as Idris collected a bottle and a glass. Each of them claimed a bottle and a glass and headed into the living room where they could drink in comfort.

Lyric was quiet and hesitant. She wanted to offer comfort, but wasn't sure how or if she should. It wasn't until Caelan nudged her and gave her a meaningful look that Lyric decided to do something.

It was good to have a friend who didn't mind helping push when you were stuck on what to do. Lyric set down the things she was carrying, then she approached Tahvo and gently took his things from him as well. He stared at her in confusion until she took his hands into hers. Despite

Idris and Caelan being there, Tahvo found himself caught up in her gaze. Before him was someone who demanded no story from him. Just simply offered a quiet support and a reminder he was not alone.

Good gods he had been acting like such a moody ass. His gaze on her softened before he closed his eyes. Forehead rested on hers as he took what she offered. He wasn't so prideful as to be embarrassed about apologizing in front of others. Pride caused enough problems in the world, and several millennia of memories backed that up.

"I did not deserve you then, Lyric and I do not deserve you now. I am sorry for my behavior. I am however grateful that you share your patience with me." He took a deep breath as he centered himself. All the hurt, doubt, and turmoil were scattering his wits and the control he clung onto. That wall he put between himself and the world had been stiff and brittle instead of malleable It had been too easy to shatter him, "If you can bear with me as I relearn how to deal with all of this, I will work to be better. It is not your job to fix me nor to walk on eggshells around me."

"You have a right to be moody. I mean in three days or something we had a date, dealt with the Greek pantheon's poster child for helicopter mothers, a creepy stalker universal sperm donor, and did an unboxing of Pandora's Box 2.0. Normal people *might* spread that nonsense out in like a month or two, not have the plot unfold in two days with little sleep and hospital visits."

"Plot?" Idris piped up, clearly amused at the two being all adorable with each other. It was admittedly nice to see his brother a little relaxed for a change, "You make it sound like we are the story in a book or something."

Caelan started laughing, "You know, I'd say life is stranger than fiction. I mean who in the world would think this stuff up? If we were a book, this would be some rather inane fourth wall breaking bordering on meta." As he spoke, he tested the bit of magic he could feel buzzing in his veins. The cork to his wine bottle popped out of the bottle and bounced across the room. So very pleased with himself, Caelan grinned in victory.

Idris snorted at his lover and offered his bottle for Caelan to open, "If we are going to go into an existential crisis about if our life and events happening are real or not, then we clearly need to consume more alcohol before we proceed."

Tahvo finally found it in himself to smile at them all. As a human he was afforded a few more freedoms in his time for a break. He just hoped that with new memories and magic did not come with a high tolerance to alcohol just yet. He so did not have enough wine to get as drunk as they all needed to be for this sort of talk.

Lyric grinned at Caelan's use of magic in opening Idris' bottle, "Well, given the past few days we've had, I think we deserve to obliterate our ability to think a bit for now and deal with it later. After a hangover and a metric ton of asprin. The world has waited thousands of years for us, it can wait a few hours longer."

"No asprin for me!" Caelan sang cheerfully, "I've got the blush!" Forgoing the glasses they had, he just chose to drink it straight from the bottle.

"Pity, I've got the red. Then again I've probably got enough painkillers still coursing through me to make this a bad idea. No one tell my doctor." Tahvo seemed amused at Caelan's antics. It looked like the demeanor of the other had picked up some oomph since his time as Amphritrite. He was far less subdued. Frankly, Tahvo hardly saw that exuberance as a bad thing.

"Drink up, Brother. I imagine we won't have time to do it later when we are hip deep in whatever shit Stephen is going to dump on us. If you have any problems, we can find you a healer or something." Idris offered oh so helpfully as he drank down his white wine.

"Drizzy, that would be you. You're the people doctor, remember?" Lyric finally willed enough magic to pop her cork out of the bottle. She watched it fly and peg Idris right in his forehead. It caused her to snort before succumbing to a fit of giggles when she saw the giant red mark in the good doctor's forehead.

"I-I'm so sorry! Sorry!" Lyric stammered through her giggles.

"No you're not. I probably did something in my past life to deserve it. Consider it your one free shot at me." Idris smirked at her. He then raised his bottle to them all, "To past lives, new starts, and less of a hula-hoop family tree."

"And to hoping we don't have the god tolerance to wine." Tahvo added, raising his own bottle after finally opening it by popping the cork into his hand. He could totally get used to having magic again, "Though the bottles aren't amethyst. So we have a higher chance of getting smashed."

"To drinking away the night then." Lyric offered as she helped toast. A calm before the storm. Some how she felt like they could all feel that impending disaster on the horizon. Yet for now she was content in pretending there was not a care in the world.

It was a nightmare to be handled later. For now they would be content in the current companionship of each other. Nightmares were easier when you had friends to face them with.

11

A couple of weeks had finally been allowed to pass peacefully. Idris decided to divorce Emily given she had vanished without contact for weeks and then finally called to tell him she was done with him. The assurance from Tahvo and Lyric that they supported him seemed to help ease his mind over the decision. He had loved Emily, but he loved the children more. The two even an offered to watch the children. No doubt the shelter dogs would love to have some willing playmates.

The shelter and clinic got back to running smoothly. The landscaping and gardening was cared for by Lyric with great pleasure. Often she had to borrow Tahvo's car to go into the city to get flowers. She took some pleasure in finding discounted wilting flowers and using her budding magic to help bring life back into them.

Fall was now in full swing, she had started realizing she needed a greenhouse on site to have plants for the winter and take care of ones she would need to transplant in the Spring. With such a goal in mind, one would often be able to find Lyric sitting on the floor of the office. That day was the same as any other as she was sitting there with drafting paper, the clinic's blueprints, and a pencil sticking out of her mouth as she chewed on it.

It was there that James found her, a smirk showing on his lips as he leaned against the doorway, "Miss Helios, have you remembered to eat today? I am in high doubts that the pencil will offer enough fiber for your diet. Perhaps if you started chewing on the drafting paper."

"Hm?" Lyric blinked slowly and tore her gaze from the designs to stare up at him. James stood with a white Styrofoam box that smelled like heaven. It was enough to make her stomach growl and remind her that she forgot to eat lunch. A stare at her phone as she saw the alarm had been dismissed. Apparently she had been really focused, "You should have been a far more worshipped god in a previous life, Mr. Cheroni."

"I had enough aggravation ferrying people from one side to another. Some of them were absolutely miserable and had a god complex that ought to have died with them. I am more than happy to be of assistance to the most benevolent queen I have ever met."

"Flattery is why some people didn't get dumped into the river." Lyric moved to dig into her pocket, "How much do I owe you?"

"Just a promise not to shove me into a river is good, thanks." James laughed as he set the box beside her and looked over the blue print and the draft paper. A thoughtful sound as he looked at the open space and also the used space, "If you put the green house between the horse runs and the clinic, it will be easier to get everything all over the property without too much aggravation." He pointed down in the one empty space, "Plus with the decks, there is an entrance near the parking lot. We can get some carts to wheel the stuff to and from."

"If we put a shed near the parking lot, we can store the rolling cart and extra supplies there." Lyric wrote down a few notes and popped the box open and picked a piece of chicken out with her fingers and ate it. Chicken fingers and fries. The easiest finger food.

James laughed at her as she just seemed to easily fall back into working. The same single-minded dedication as Tah-vo. Both had been a formidable pair back then and just as dedicated as they were now. Lyric's choice in name had been entertaining. While she could be affectionate and gentle to souls she saw as weary or in need of redemption, there had been no kindness spared for those full of pride, hatred, and cruelty. No one could accuse of Persephone for being a weak pushover. Her name became a whispered curse among those who were afraid to be destined for Tartarus. Hades had no qualms about letting Persephone be the judge of who went where. When she was in the Underworld, her word had been law.

Frankly, he could not have served a better Queen. James watched her work for a few more moments before looking out towards the run, "I'll be unleashing the hounds shortly. So might want to wrap up."

"Mhm." Lyric nodded and made a few more notes as she nibbled on her chicken. After a moment she started to stack the blueprint onto the drafting paper and rolled it up. A rubber band to hold it all together was stretched over it as she started to clean, "I hope they ate already. Else they will try stealing my lunch."

"Spot is a bottomless pit. He will try to butter you up for it anyway. Now he can actually sweet talk you for it." James said. A grin pulled on his cheeks as he watched her tuck everything away into the closet space, balancing her food in one hand.

"Yeah well, he is a growing dog. Still. He's been getting bigger and it isn't just his belly. Though thankfully he hasn't sprouted any new heads yet."

James laughed at that. The three heads tended to get a little snappy at each other once in a while. One head was sometimes better than two or three. Easier to feed at any rate. He started for the sliding doors, adjusting his jacket as he did so. A frown as he peered outside and the storm front on the edge of the horizon. Just looking at it flashing and sparking had him on edge. Something felt... off.

"Maybe we should keep the dogs in the indoor run today." He murmured quietly, causing Lyric to come over and stare out the window too.

"I'll go check on the dogs, let Tahvo know to keep an ear out. I feel like... the storm has dread behind it... like Stephen." Lyric admitted quietly. The feeling was the same as those times Stephen had ever been around. An unease that chilled her to her bones. Given they hadn't heard from Stephen or even Emily for a while, she had no doubt this could be something of their doing.

James nodded to her, but lingered, unwilling to leave her alone. He had only been somewhat near Stephen and the man had been unconscious so he didn't get a feel for the magic. He trusted Lyric with her gut feeling and started for the door, "Check on the horses after. Call ahead and see if Sylvia is out there yet." It would ensure she was not alone at least.

"Can do." She murmured, eyes on the large stormfront. Her fingers ran over the fading burn scars on her hands.

Finally, Lyric willed herself to go down the hall and frowned as she neared it. The dogs were being far louder than usual. Something was clearly upsetting them. As soon as she entered, Lyric nearly got trampled by Spot as he tried to bolt out the door. Her hand went out like a flash to grab onto his collar to keep him from plowing into the wall head first.

"Cerberus! Calm down before you get a concussion."

Cerberus let out a low snarl as he stopped moving. Teeth were bared viciously as he lowered his head. Shoulders were hunched and he glared down towards the end of the hall.

"I need to get to Tahvo" Cerberus said, voice taking on a deepness she was familiar with when he was a far larger beast.

The snarl in the voice made Lyric worry, "He is with someone, Cerberus. Let's just check on the other dogs. Tahvo will be fine."

"The dogs are fine." Cerberus bit off the words. Short little growled accents as his throat rumbled. Then there was a moment of a low whine that escaped. He needed his Tahvo as much as Tahvo needed him.

Lyric's eyes widened and she slowly released his collar. Worry gnawed at her gut and she fought to keep a clear head. They couldn't afford to make mistakes if their were lives in danger. Lyric was not going to doubt Cerberus if he really felt something was wrong.

"Fine, but be careful. I am going to find Sylvia and check on the horses."

Cerberus gave a sharp nod before bolting down the hall. The scrape of claws echoing as Lyric nearly wanted to follow after him. She wanted to make sure Tahvo was okay too but... he wasn't alone. James and Cerberus would make sure he was alright. Maybe she needed to try to call Cecilia.

Lyric made sure to check on all of the dogs anyway. Assuring herself they truly were all just worked up. The hounds were loud, filling the space with echoing sounds that just felt like more were there than accounted for. Lyric tried to soothe them, but a rumbling thunder just made it worse. A deep breath as she promised to return. Then, she walked as quickly as she could. Lyric hesitated as the power flickered. Another few steps and she could hear the humming sound of power fluctuating loudly before a surge. A shudder of the air as the lights dimmed down and then got brighter. It made her hesitate to take another step as it felt like a warning.

There was an urgent need to check on Sylvia, but at the same time she didn't know if she should stay to ensure everyone else was safe. Cerberus had gone to Tahvo, but she worried if Stephen was going to target him again. A frown and she forced herself to trust the strength of the others and made it to the office and started dialing on the phone. A frown as the phone rang and wasn't picked up.

After a few more rings she heard the voicemail pick up. As she waited to record a message, the power surged hard again with a drowning vwoom that made her entire body shiver right before a crashing sound that deafened her. The lights suddenly glowed bright with a vibrating shudder and a loud screech of a massive power surge and all of the lights exploded. Light fixtures rained down glass and sparks before everything went dark.

Lyric dove down with a scream as she tried to hide under the desk. Her head rang and felt like cotton was in her ears. She trembled as looked through the blinding blotches into the darkened room. Despite the dark clouds outside, there was a faint grey light that let her see vague shapes in the room. Her body trembled as she forced herself to climb out, trying not to put her hands in the fine glass.

She needed to make sure everyone else was alright! Lyric dug around the desk for her cell phone and frowned when there was no signal. Wordless cursing and she began to look around her desk only to find the corded phone on the desk in pieces. That certainly wasn't normal. Lyric went to the closet and got her coat out and pulled it on. James and Cerberus were with Tahvo so she knew they would be okay. At least that was what she was telling herself. Sylvia was alone and Lyric felt dread at the realization.

That feeling drove her as she went out the back and ran down along the deck. The air was dry and she felt her hair stand on end as though surrounded by static. The feeling of impending doom increased with every step as she ran. Her stomach knotting as she threw open the gate from the run and latched it behind her before taking off at a dead run for the stables. Her lungs burned and made the destination seem that much further. Gods, she really needed to start running more often.

When she finally reached the stables, she could hear the whinnies and panic of the horses inside. Lyric was gasping for air as she grabbed at the barn door and tried to open it.

Her heart dropped down into her stomach and she yanked harder. There wasn't any give to the door, it just acted as though it were immovable stone.

"Sylvia! Sylvia!" Lyric tried to shake the door harder before hitting it with her hand. Dammit! It wasn't opening! She started to go around the barn to one of the side doors and it was the same.

Fists pounded on the door as she yelled the woman's name over the sound of thunder. Her skin crawled when she started feeling *something* in the air. A loud shout at the door and she kicked it. A curse as she felt pain shoot up her leg from pulling that stupid stunt. A look over the building as she could see the rolling clouds twisting and churning up above them. It was starting to blot out the remaining light and make it as dark as death's robes. Flashes of illumination as the lightning crashed above and thunder boomed making her ache. At least there were no exploding lightbulbs this time. Especially as it looked like the ones that normally would light the area were already shattered and rained sparks.

There had to be a way to get inside somehow. Especially as there had to be a reason for the stables to be sealed like this. Lyric racked her brain for any clues as to why this would be a focal point. Especially for Stephen of all people. She knew most of the gods had their own horses. Mainly stemmed from the four that pulled Zeus' chariot. Did they unknowingly have the wind-gods disguised as horses or were they just the unfortunate victims in being trapped in the epicenter of Stephen's plans.

What type of magic was being used? Maybe she could use her own magic to break in. Would hers be strong enough? Cosmos above help her. She prayed silently that she could get in. Sylvia and the horses were in danger and gods only knew who else was possibly in there. She took a deep breath and pressed her hand against the unmoving door and focused.

That energy she felt every time she did magic churned and twisted in her chest and through her veins as though it were as much a part of her as her blood. Under her feet, the ground felt as though it was swelling and becoming like water as she felt the Earth move and ripple.

Softly she pleaded to the Earth, "Please. *Please* help me now. I have to keep people safe." It rippled and she sank down to the ground more. Focusing. Willing as she could feel the air around her start to crackle. There was the feeling of impending doom filling her heart and she knew if she didn't figure this out soon, they would be harmed or worse. Lyric reached down to the dirt below her and touched it, "I know I do not ask for very much. I haven't in a long time, but I need you to work with me." She usually only did gardening, but now she was fighting a power that felt so much stronger than her own. Yet... she knew she could not just stand around. She needed to fight.

The ground started to twist under her. It was forming rough shapes as it rose to meet her fingers on the door. A grim smile and Lyric looked up and pressed harder against the door that was magicked shut to see if it would give. She could do this. She encouraged the earth underfoot to start pushing up under the wood. To force it to put pressure along the bottom edge. At first the wood started to creak. Then it started to crack and splinter and Lyric panicked. Should she run? What if she let go? Dammit, if she stopped now she would never get in!

She had to use the earth. Lyric refocused and coaxed the dirt and stone. It was slow moving, but it formed a layer between herself and the door. The wood crackled and buckled as she forced it to push against the bottom of the door. There was a loud crash of thunder and lightning that made her ears ring and vision blur. Everything was dark except the flashes of light as everything boomed over them. This was taking too long!

"Hurry up!" Lyric yelled, forcing as much of her will into the magic as possible. The door finally buckled entirely and exploded inward, but she had not accounted for the wall around it. Wood exploded and cracked around and she let out a little shriek as she pressed against the tiny dirt shield in an effort to avoid the wood shrapnel. Arms covered her head, letting the dirt shower down like water and covering her with uprooted soil. She spit out the dirt and wood bits as she wiped at her eyes. If she thought the outside was loud and dark, the inside was even worse.

Lyric took a breath and forced herself to stand. Legs trembled as she entered. The horses were slamming around their stalls, trying to escape. A step in and her foot hit something right as it sank into something that gave a soft squelch underfoot. Blinking a little, Lyric knelt down and tried to see what her foot had hit. It was soft and luke-warm to the touch. After a moment of feeling around she realized it was a person when her hands came away sticky and wet from trying to feel for a heartbeat.

Right then, lightning flashed outside and Lyric could see the after images of who she touched. She screamed and backpedaled against a stall door, staring at the pitchfork that stuck out of her body as lightening flashed. Wide eyes bore into her and showed the emptiness of death and a face twisted by agony. Suddenly Lyric felt like she couldn't breathe. Head spun she tried to sort her panic and focus. Why would *he* have done this? Deep down, Lyric understood why, but right now her mind scrambled at someone she knew murdered. Was Stephen still there? Was he going to do anything else? The horses were in danger too!

Questions fled as soon as they came when Lyric's hair was grabbed and she was hauled off her feet. Suddenly she was screaming and kicking as hard as she could at the source. Nails clawed at the hand gripping her. Finally her foot connected with something hard enough and she was dropped. She blindly ran through the darkness. Then she tripped over Sylvia's body and slammed into a support beam. In a frantic effort to keep moving she spun from the momentum to put as much distance between her and the one who grabbed her.

"I see you've been practicing your magic. Too little, too late really. Should have killed me when you had the chance." Stephen's voice drifted in the darkness, "Then again, I would never accuse you of being terribly swift, after all you got tricked into having my child."

"You trick everyone into having your child! It isn't new for you. If it had legs and a pulse, you tried to screw it." Lyric snarled. Finally she found the ladder to the loft. She started to climb, hoping she could find something up there to help. Splinters bit into her hands as they slid to keep hold of the ladder in the dark. Her eyes hurt from the strain of trying to see a damned thing. When there was no more ladder for her to grab onto, she felt around for the loft and was met with more wood and pieces of hay. Happy for a solid surface, she crawled on and kept moving until she bumped her head against the wall.

"Yet no one else found it necessary to murder an entire pantheon. Which included *my* son."

"You took my son!" Lyric yelled, "You stole him away from me because he treated Hades like the father that he should have been. You *took him from us* and then you poisoned him with your selfishness!"

"I SAVED HIM!" Stephen bellowed, shaking the stables and it was followed by a deafening boom, yet his voice persisted through the storm, "And who is to say the great and mighty Persephone, Queen of the Underworld, is not selfish? You let the world wither and die half of the year just to be with my brother. If your mother had not demanded your return, the world would be barren and dead. It would be your fault."

Lyric balled up her splintered hands, letting the pain give her focus. He was trying to goad her into coming after him. Breaths were shallow as she centered herself, "My mother was *selfish*. She decided to punish the world because she couldn't keep me within arm's reach. I made my *choice* to remain with Hades. I would done so again with circumstances different I will do so again."

Gods, she wished she could tell where Stephen was. Her hearing was hindered by the pounding of her heart and her breathing all too hard. It was difficult to do much more than panic. Head thumped back against the wall and she tried to listen. Tried to hear or even see better. Yet, as soon as she thought she could move, thunder clapped loud enough to make her ears ring and lightening flashed bright enough to ruin her night vision all over again.

It seemed too quiet. Did he leave? It made no sense but... she shifted then to move slow. Cautiously she began to crawl through the straw to find something to use to defend herself. For all she knew, she just couldn't hear him over everything else. Now that magic was involved, it changed so much.

The moment the ladder creaked, Lyric started scrambling. She needed a weapon! Anything at all! A curse was spat out when she hit her arm on the pointed tines of something. Lyric blindly grabbed for it and all she was rewarded with was the loud scrape of a handle against wood and a clattering thunk as it fell off the loft. Shit!

"Lyric?"

A soft voice made her freeze. Eyes stared wide in the dark at the direction of the impossible voice, "Sylvia?"

"Lyric, help me! I'm hurt! It hurts so much!" The woman's voice sobbed, "I can't see you. I think I am on a ladder."

Lyric stared towards the voice and started moving towards it before she stopped herself, "I saw you! You were dead!"

"I was just pretending! Lyric, please! How did you get in here? I heard an explosion!" The voice sounded soft and scared. Trembling words that Lyric didn't trust at all.

"I... it doesn't matter. How are the horses?" Lyric asked, slowly moving and she got closer to the source of the voice. She was trying to gather the willpower to use magic before something felt wrong. Lyric tried to keep low as the feeling grew worse. Then an iron grip clamped onto her arm and ripped her from the loft.

Lyric hauled from the loft with a scream and released mid-arc. She crashed down onto the hard ground with a sickening crack that she was sure was bone, but everything hurt so badly it was hard to tell which part of her it was. She gasped for air. Pain blinded her more than the darkness and she was whimpering as she tried to find a foothold in her thoughts. The horses started kicking at the stall doors and she swore the storm outside was louder than before. Or maybe that was the way her head felt when she tried to move. Her left wrist felt like fire engulfed it as she tried to move and her brain felt like it was swimming as she tried sitting up. Then white flashed behind her eyes and she swore breathlessly.

As if the eight foot drop hadn't been enough, her pain drowned out the sound of feet. Which had not allowed her to prepare for the air that left her lungs as she was kicked in the chest. The force knocked her onto her back and she wheezed. Gods she hoped the others were having a better time than this. While she wanted help, she didn't want them endangered by demented asshole either. A weight was on her throat suddenly, making her gasp reflexively. She began to make a choking sound as she tried to thrash at the boot. One hand uselessly flopped against it, pain shooting up her arm while the other hand gripped at what felt like leather.

"You know, I was trying to get my horses back. One of them was just so stubborn. He decided death was a better option than to be mine again. Pity given they were once powerful gods. Yet they didn't want anything to do with power." A tsking sound and Stephen glared down, "We were *immortal*, Persephone. Invincible! Powers beyond the greatest imagination. Nature bowed down to our will! We were worshipped! Yet you! You and my brother destroyed it all! And for what purpose? To live these *pathetic* mortal lives? Just to keep my child out of my hands?"

The weight shifted and she could *almost* breathe until he pressed down again and glared at her. The flicker of a yellow light in his eyes was not from the outside storm, but from his powers, "You must not have loved him very much if you thought his death was preferable to our survival."

Another crash of thunder, drowned out the words that Lyric barely heard. What she had heard was a distinct crack of wood. Something thumped and then another crack. Then another. Then another, the thumps becoming louder as she watched Stephen jerk. His eyes going towards the source of the sound seconds before a horse barreled forward and reared back. The upswing of its limbs knocked Stephen off her. Lyric panicked, wiggling to roll so she would not get trampled. The legs came down so fast and she closed her eyes, waiting for more pain. Instead the feet landed on either side of her, leaving her under the arch of the torso.

Its snout moved to press against her face. Nipping at her cheek with its mouth. A breath felt like an eternity, but Lyric soon felt the painful fog clear to a dull ache. Her vision swam at only the edges. A blink up at the sable-black horse and she reached to pet it, careful to not poke its eye. Was she suddenly seeing better in the dark?

"Thank you." She rasped softly, "Orphnaeus?"

"No thanks, you came to help us." The horse responded gently, "Yes, I am he. Though I prefer Oreo. Those taste better." He attempted with a light tone.

"You have always cared for us, our Queen." A glance towards the groaning god he knocked back. "Even when you did not know for whom you cared for. Do you wish for us to remain to assist you?"

Lyric sat up and considered the horse. Help would be nice but... "Did he kill Sylvia?"

The head dipped down, shame evident, "Yes, I am afraid we could not save her in time."

"It is not your fault." Lyric assured him. Honestly, perhaps anyone else would be more startled by talking horses, but she had been a Greek Goddess. Memories she clung to now as she remembered the all too fresh pain of things Zeus had done. The first time she had to leave Hades after their first six months together. The losses. The feeling of questioning her own mind.

Lyric remembered all too well who she was. Her name was not spoken with sweetness and soft giggles when she was the goddess. Not always. No... she had chosen that name for a reason. After a few breaths, she finally made a move to stand up as. A look to her very weak wrist, "Is the storm to keep him trapped on the property?"

"Yes. He was trying to take his steeds and the rest of us with him last time. He wishes to draw us out of our mortal shells." By killing them, but they weren't having any of that nonsense. Unfortunately, one of the steeds had been drawn out, thus the ravaging storm. "It was a wind god that had been killed previously. When Zeus had returned, the god had made sure that he could not escape. Though it had been unable to prevent further harm."

Any intention to respond was lost when she heard a growl from a beast. Her heart raced again as she focused ahead. Aching pain pushed to the back of her mind. Focus, Lyric reminded herself that she needed to focus. She stepped forward as the growl became louder, "Get the others out! Go anywhere but here!" She ordered.

The horse hesitated before she looked at him with a look that told him not to question her. That sweet and easily frightened nature seemed to have turned cold and her eyes had become dark. The air crackled around her. Then there was a loud click and the stomping of horses had doors swinging open.

Her next words echoed in the barn, "Go! Now!"

The thunder of outside was drowned out by the stampeding of horses to the hole she had created in the barn earlier. The monstrous growl continued, and Lyric stared into the black. Her eyes were adjusted to it now. Her name had once been a choice she had made. She had chosen to remain with Hades. She had chosen her name. Right now, she would make the choice to face Stephen alone. Before he harmed others.

"I was..." She grit her teeth, "I *am* Persephone. I am the once Queen of the Underworld. I ruled. I judged. I aided Hades in your punishment for your hubris! You are no longer worthy of the name of Zeus, for the glory that once held has been tarnished by your very actions." She took another step forward. The shadows themselves seemed to have shifted before her. Something massive and glared at her with sickly yellow eyes that glowed.

Shadows moved again, now looming over her to the point where she had to crane her neck to look up at it. Lyric may have practiced at magic, but combat against a being like that was something far out of her realm of practice in this life. The fear wormed its way into her thoughts and then was ignored vehemently. Instead she glared up at it defiantly. There was no choice, she had to deal with this beast. A short lived act as she was swiped by a massive paw. The motion was too fast for her to react to except to have been sent through the wooden wall of the barn. Splinters scattered and dug into her skin as she braced for when she hit the ground hard and tumbled. Pain shot through her body again then eased as the last couple of tumbles felt more rolling into a plush blanket. The Earth gently cradled her, allowing her to collect her thoughts again.

Damn it, he was faster and stronger than she was. She pushed herself up and shuddered as she ached all over again. It was as though Orphnaeus had done nothing at all. Lyric looked up in time to see the entire wall bow out before breaking the rest of the way. Her arms came up to shelter herself from the debris with an earthen shield. The beast was nearly as tall as the barn was at the shoulder. Lightening illuminated the area fully as there was a crack and crashing sound as it touched ground somewhere. Rain soaked its fur as it brought itself to its full height. A wolf with fur black as the abyss and eyes pale and furious started to claw into the dirt, ready to attack. A snarl tore from its mouth with teeth bared as he launched himself at Lyric.

Lyric ignored her panic and she focused on the Earth that seemed willing to respond to her now. A wall of mud came up like a wave to crash into the massive wolf. As soon as there was impact, she was running to her left. Clumps of mud flew as the hound shook it off. She preferred Cerberus when it came to giant dogs. Oh how she would love having one now.

The wolf shook and then took off after his prey. Two bounds and he quickly had overtaken her as he slid into her path. A snarl before he snapped at her. She dipped her fingers into the ground as though it were water and followed through. Instead of meat and blood, he received a mouthful of dirt and rocks. With him subdued for another breath, she pivoted on a foot and zigged to her right.

Thoughts raced through her mind. That had to be Stephen! That had to be his foul magic! There was no telling what would happen if she outright killed him. Would he just reincarnate? Would he even stay dead? Was anyone even ruling the Underworld? After all, she could not tell if everyone had been reincarnated or not. Such thoughts roared through her mind like a tsunami. She felt the ground tremble as he closed in behind her.

She ducked down as the Earth came over her like a massive bowl when Stephen got close. It shook and dirt was knocked loose down onto her when he crashed into it. Then she could hear him digging for her. Very slowly she crawled out from under the bowl through a gap.

"Lyric!"

She froze. Eyes widened in fear when that scratching against her earthen shield ceased. No no no. No!

"Tahvo!" She screamed his name, "Run!" Lyric scampered out in time to be overshadowed by the wolf leaping over and bounding towards Tahvo. She started clawing at the dirt to get onto her feet. Mud and grass wedged under her nails as she was on all fours for a few feet. The wolf blocked her view of Tahvo and the world slowed down then.

Feet tangled under her, causing her to crash down and land hard. Eyes were wide as she forced herself to look up to see as much as she could. The wolf reared its head back with its maw parted. She screamed until her voice gave out. Fists slammed into the ground and there was loud booming crack that echoed and a wail of pain that seemed to have silenced even the storm. The stench of blood was all she could smell and the hound's head was down and mouth obscured.

What happened?! Lyric gasped for air as her lungs burned. In fact all of her felt like it was on fire. Oh it hurt, but the idea of Tahvo dead hurt so much more. There was so much more she wanted to learn about him. To share. Tears blinded her as she tried to drag her body across the ground to them. They were so far from her. So far.

Oh gods. The dark mass lit up as thunder cracked over them and lightening followed soon after. Something strange and twisted stuck out from the front of Stephen. A glistening crimson spire in the storm that was burned in her vision.

She needed to know Tahvo's fate. Lyric tried to push herself up, but she hurt far too much. The woman had pushed herself far past her limit and every attempt made her body burn more. Everything was on fire and that alone made her vision blur. She did not care. She had to see! Something dark moved by the wolf. Damn it, did Stephen live?! Wait! The form looked like a person... the wolf was vanishing. Perhaps she failed...

The thunder was softening in its sound. Although... Lyric wondered if that was just the sound of her heart. Perhaps... if Tahvo had died then she would be with him. The next time around she could be with him without the past hunting them down. Such a pretty last thought before pain and unconsciousness swallowed her.

12

Her whole body ached. It was the first thought Lyric had when she snapped into consciousness. She felt as though her skin was covered in a horrible sunburn. Everywhere. There were things she did not know could hurt before that now did. The unpleasant feeling let her know that she was alive. Maybe.

All she saw was darkness and that immediately caused a surge of panic. Her eyes blinked in an effort to focus on anything, but she saw no shapes. No light. Nothing. Then she tried to work her voice. That one didn't want to work at first either. It was as though she had not spoken in centuries. Then there was a crack of sound that did not sound human. Her throat hurt at the attempt, but she tried again anyway.

"Tahvo!" She tried to call out his name, but it sounded muffled. Why was everything dark?! She pawed at herself to try to understand her surroundings. Her fingers felt heavy and bulky. Something thick covered her torso... her arms... neck. She patted her way up to her face. Her nose stuck out just enough for air. Her covered nails clawed at the fabric on her face. Immediately she regretted the act the moment the dim light filtering through the blinds hit her eyes. A grimace as she closed her eyes tight. Breathing was ragged at that new spike of pain lacerating her skull that made the rest of her hurt by extension. She gasped for air as she forced her way to freedom from the fabric.

Then she chanced opening her eyes just a crack. A look down at the wrapping on her upper body and she frowned. Greek writing on the bandages to promote healing? At least that was what the whispers in her mind told her. A long stare at the braided golden bands on her wrists over the bandages. Lyric was not sure where in the world those came from. Maybe when her brain caught up with the rest of her consciousness, she would remember.

The bandages though... inscriptions of healing and a strengthening of... something about containment. No... that wasn't right. A deep frown and she pushed back the thick plush blankets to see her entire body had been wrapped with the utmost care. The writing as precise as possible, though she could see in places it had become weak. As though fear and worry nearly tainted the inten- tion. Lyric looked up and called out again, "Tahvo?" Her cracking voice held an edge of panic. Was she dead? Alive? Her head hurt. She knew the dead could feel pain, else the punishments for the wicked would not have worked in Tartarus.

Silence. Lyric frowned at the door. Then the room itself. It was her room in his house. For, as Tahvo put it, when she wished for privacy from him. She never used it during her stay. She much preferred his scent near her. Her heart lurched at the thought of him dead and she trembled. She failed him. He was gone. Why would the Fates be so cruel as to leave her without him in the world beside her? Was it not already a cruelty to have her separated from him six months of every year of their past?

It hurt like hell, but she forced herself to swing her legs off the bed and dangle over the side. Ow. She ground her teeth and pushed herself up onto her feet. Then she pushed off the bed and the moment legs had to support her, they folded under her. Weak limbs caused her to yelp as she crashed unceremoniously onto the floor. There was a pained curse and tears pricked at the corners of her eyes. Anger flooded her as well as grief. She was alone. She had failed.

Lyric began sob, her voice cracking with broken wails that were interspersed with whines of pain. She couldn't hear the thundering steps of so many feet rushing upstairs. The first set of feet that burst into the room belonged to Spot. He whined as he started licking Lyric's face with an affectionate fervor. Then Asteri, who nudged Spot out of the way to begin licking at her human's face as well. Trying to get rid of all of those tears.

Then heavier footsteps and a gasp before the owner ran over. Soft voice ushering the excited hounds as the owner moved to gently move the woman into their arms. Lyric rolled her head as it was cradled and stared into loving green eyes. Panic shone in them as much as relief. Suddenly her vision blurred again as she started crying. Overwhelmed by pain and emotion as she reached up towards him. Pawing at the air and his head to feel him until his hand covered hers and pressed her palm against his cheek.

"I am here, Lyric. I promise to every shadow and star and I am here." Tahvo told her softly. He leaned down and kissed her cheek. Salty tears no doubt stung the raw skin. He pulled her closer to his body, "I had feared you would never awaken again. I had seen you being chased. Then the wolf was dead. Then you.... Marco and James had seen you in the Underworld." His brother was dead. It had been months to deal with that loss of a sibling and the woman he came to love. Both were painful and yet he knew one death had been needed. "I saw you..." He trailed off as he pressed his face against her hair.

When Lyric had laid that killing blow, she had looked like the very scorched Earth itself. As though she had become it to destroy the wolf. Her body had crackled with destructive magic that had long laid dead. Whatever had helped her summon that magic had left with the storm. A swift wind... and yet that mortal body had not been enough to contain the sheer destructive power it held.

In his arms was no longer a mortal woman, but a goddess. One who balanced on the very edge of true death, but Cecilia had helped him figure out a way to save her from the brink. They had wrapped the Earthen body. They had used old magic and hoped it worked. Prayers... magic...

hell he had started creating an altar of a small scale that resembled those of old.

Whatever had happened to make this work, he was glad, "It has been… it has been six months." He told her as he tried to soothe her and banish those tears. That news seemed to startle her. Even as he said it, he realized the importance and he just looked at her in awe.

Lyric hiccupped and then made a sound of pain from it. A look up to him. A slow breath in and then out to prepare for the effort it took to speak, "I hope… that does not become a trend. I would not like waking up in pain. Or falling. Definitely not every six months. My heart already died every Spring once before."

Tahvo stared and then laughed weakly, "I shall make sure I am the next one to fry myself if this indeed has become our fate once more. Although not for another half year." He promised softly. His hand slid along her bandaged arm that he had inscribed. The tears shed in grief had long been absorbed. Every day he added more. Filling in every available space as he saw fit. He dipped down to touch his forehead against hers, dark hair fell down to hide them from the dim light, "I have so very much to tell you. So very much to fill you in on. So much lost time to make up for, both in this life and our last."

A shuddering breath, his panic crawling up to seize his throat shut. *Please, let the Fates be kind. I have paid in blood and mind for my heart to beat again. I do not wish for history to repeat. I have sought to fight against such an outcome.* He prayed silently. Something he did not realize the goddess in his arms could hear.

"I do not think history will repeat again." Lyric responded automatically. Not realizing she heard his prayer. He went still and stared down at her. He looked so scared. Then she curled her hand against his face and slid it to the back of his neck and gently pulled him down to her until his lips were a breath from hers, "I do not think we are bound to the compromise of the past. It is something I will have paid for the last time."

"Lyric, I do not wish to lose you again. You are the first goddess returned to our pantheon." He had not quite earned the title of god yet. Though over the months he had felt that power grow. He was not sure if Zeus would return fully fledged as well. With his defeat by Persephone's hand, would that change things? Perhaps Persephone would rule their pantheon in Zeus' stead.

Tahvo closed his eyes, "I do not know if I shall ever be granted such a thing, but if you will have me, I wish to earn your love properly. Day by day learning your loves and hates. I wish to learn not of Persephone, but of Lyric Helios. I fear we have had little time that was not wrought with chaos. May I please properly earn your love and one day share my heartbeat with yours?"

Lyric shuddered and closed her eyes. She was a goddess. That fact resonated through her to prove truth to his words. He spoke as though in soft worship of her. A smile and she gently graced his lips with her own. Gentle and yet stinging. She gently let him draw away from her and she looked up at him. Wonder and love for him, but he was right. In this life they had barely enough time to get to know each other. Not as much as she wanted to.

"Then if you wish to know of the heart and soul of Lyric Helios, I wish to know the heart and soul of Tahvo Melanthios just as thoroughly. I want to learn of it while at your side. I will need to learn what it means to be a goddess here and perhaps one day you will join me. With far less dying and bandages."

Lyric smiled up at him, ignoring the pain, "I will have you, Tahvo. I made the choice to end our world and start over. I make this choice to be at your side. No one will ever choose that for me. It has always been me and you, my King, have long earned my love."

The End.

The Story Will Continue

In Two Coins.

Coming Soon